HAWK:
FOOL'S GOLD

Jared Hawk didn't go looking for a fight, but when the Mexican called him out he killed the pistolero. He didn't know the Mexican's brother, Luis Brava, headed an outlaw gang until he took his revenge, and left Hawk to die. That was a mistake—Hawk didn't die that easy, and now he was looking for his own personal vengeance!

WILLIAM S. BRADY

HAWK: FOOL'S GOLD

Complete and Unabridged

LINFORD
Leicester

First published in Great Britain 1980 by
Fontana Books,
London

First Large Print Edition
published April 1985
by arrangement with
Fontana Books,
London

British Library CIP Data

Brady, William S.
  Fool's gold.—Large print ed.—
  (Hawk; no. 5)—(Linford Western library)
  I. Title   II. Series
  823'.914[F]   PR6052.R262/

  ISBN 0-7089-6085-5

Published by
F. A. Thorpe (Publishing) Ltd.
Anstey, Leicestershire
Set by Rowland Phototypesetting Ltd.
Bury St. Edmunds, Suffolk
Printed and bound in Great Britain by
T. J. Press (Padstow) Ltd., Padstow, Cornwall

For Jane Harkett,
who always puts us at the front.

1

INSIDE the cantina the air was cool. Beaded curtains held out most of the light, filling the interior with shadow so that the farthest corners were dark, impenetrable. It was quiet, the only sounds the lazy buzzing of the flies and the occasional chink of bottle against glass. A faint odour of chili mingled with the redolence of tobacco smoke and spilled beer and sweat, those smells gradually overcome by the sharper tang of the lye soap the barkeep was using on the floor.

He was a man well into his middle years, the fruits of his profession beginning to swell his belly outwards over the dirty apron he wore. He worked in silence, concentrating on the planks, keeping his eyes down as though seeking out every offending stain. At regular intervals he jerked his head back, flicking a cowlick of greasy brown hair from his eyes and darting them round to glance at the shadowy corner where the solitary drinker was working his way steadily through a bottle.

The man had come in around mid-afternoon—no one in Cabanos bothered over much about exact time-keeping—and asked for food and whisky. The cantina had been quiet then, the noonday rush finished and the evening drinking not yet begun. For no particular reason, the barkeep had been grateful the man was alone: there was something about him that suggested suppressed tension, an aura of controlled violence. He was not a cowboy. The barkeep, long-practised in guessing a man's occupation from his clothes and demeanour, identified him instantly as a gunfighter, a pistoleer. He was young—in his twenties to judge by his face, which was leanly-planed, good-looking save for its hardness. His eyes were grey and cold, scanning the room with automatic caution from under the brim of a low-crowned black hat that matched the sombre shade of his pants and leather vest. His right hand stayed close to the butt of the Colt's .45 Frontier model sitting snug and deadly in the cutaway holster on his right hip. The barkeep had studied the gunbelt with surreptitious interest: it was unusual to see a custom-made belt, and this one was doubly interesting. The revolver holster was integral with the belt, the scabbard riveted in place so that the muzzle was angled slightly forwards, the butt canted back for a fast draw. It was matched on the left side by a similar rig that was even more unusual: it held a 10-gauge Meteor shotgun, the single barrel cut down to no more than twelve inches and the stock cut to a pistol grip that jutted forwards, cross-draw fashion.

When the man picked up his glass, the barkeep saw that he used his left hand and knew he was a shootist. He also saw that the man wore a black leather glove on his hand, held tight in place by a drawstring around the cuff. At first the barkeep thought he might be one of the fancy kids who fanned their guns because they hadn't worked up the nerve to rely on a single

3

shot. That might have explained the scattergun. But then he noticed the fingers of the man's left hand were stiff, unable to close properly on the whisky glass so that he used his thumb to hold the thing in place against his palm; and changed his mind.

When the man dropped a coin on the bar and took his bottle over to the corner —where he was protected on two sides by the angles of the walls and almost hidden in the shadow—the barkeep knew he was no punk kid.

The man was called Jared Hawk. He was a hired gun.

He was in Cabanos because it was mid-way between Terra Alta and Valverde. And Valverde was the closest town he could think of with a bank and a post office. In Terra Alta he had killed two men with bounties posted on them, collecting a note from the marshal that was worth two hundred and fifty dollars in any American bank. The reward brought his money up to close on one thousand dollars.

He needed the post office to arrange the transfer of the money to Iowa.

He thought about Iowa as he drank his whisky and stared idly at the door . . .

Farm country . . .

Corn country . . .

The harvest would be in now . . . The nights clear and mellow with that big silver moon shining over the stubble . . .

His mother—Mary Hawk—and his little brother, Jamey, were running the farm. He had been ever since Jared went back.

Went back and killed his father.

Instinctively, he rubbed at his gloved hand, trying to flex the fingers rendered near useless by the pitchfork his drunken father had rammed through the palm. He had quit home after that, sickened by his father's drinking and the frequent beatings; knowing that if he stayed it had to come to a final confrontation. He had wandered around after his hand healed, concealing his disfigurement under the black glove. Had become a mule-skinner;

a scout; a lawman, working with Bill Hickok. Had learned to use a gun with deadly efficiency. And learned that he enjoyed its usage.

Then he had met the truth of something Hickok told him:

"It don't matter he's yore father. You can't afford to leave enemies behind you. Men in our line of work, they need to watch their backs. You go home an' settle things."

Jared had gone back. Nothing had changed much. His father was still drunk and still mean. The big difference was that this time Caleb Hawk had tried to use a shotgun instead of a pitchfork.

Jared had killed him.

And ridden away, knowing that he was never going home again.

He had wandered west and south, drifting down into Texas and New Mexico. Teamed up with a gunfighter called John T. McLain. A man near old enough to be his father, and more like a father than Caleb had ever been. McLain had taught him a lot. And when he died in a dirty little street fight that blew up for no particular reason and left the older man spilling his life into the dust of a dirty little street in a dirty little town, McLain had wished the scattergun and the belt on Jared.

Jared had worn it since. Had used the Meteor to avenge McLain's killing, and devoted himself to doing what he knew best. It was a dangerous life, but he enjoyed it. It payed better than cowboying or skinning mule teams, and the discipline of scouting for the Army rubbed against the wild streak in him. And it kept him moving, seldom affording him the time to pick over the scabs of guilt that still remained. In that direction, his one concession was to send money home: whatever he made, he sent most of it back to Iowa. He no longer wrote letters; just sent the money from places all over the western states and territories, never halting long enough at any one place that a reply might catch up with him.

He preferred it that way: any other might hurt too much.

"I hope you understand, Ma. I know Jamey does."

Hawk lifted his glass and tossed the whisky down his throat. The liquor burned and he took a swallow of tepid beer to kill the fire. Then he ran his right hand over the stubble covering his jaw and realized that he hadn't shaved in two days. It had been longer since he took a bath.

He stood up and called the barkeep.

"You got a tub? An' a room?"

"Sure." The barkeep nodded. "Got a room out back. Tub in the outhouse. Room's thirty cents a night, bath'll be twenty."

Hawk dropped a dollar on the table. "Change should cover the stable."

"Yeah." The barkeep grounded his mop in the bucket. "Want me to put yore horse away?"

Hawk shook his head: "No. I'll look after him myself."

"Yore choice, mister." The barkeep made no move to pick up the coin. It was as though he wanted to stay as far away from Hawk as possible. "Stable's right next to the outhouse."

"Thanks." Hawk corked the bottle and fastened his left hand around the neck. "How long?"

For a moment, the barkeep looked confused. Then he understood the question and said, "I'll get the water now. Won't be long."

Hawk nodded and went out through the door on to the street.

Cabanos was still in the muggy heat of late afternoon. Off to the north, where the high ground flanking the Rio Grande lifted up towards the sky, thunderheads were forming, building a curtain of dark grey and black against the blue of late summer. The settlement was hunched like a nervous animal under the threat of the storm, the single-storey buildings flanking the main street along its two-hundred-yard length seeming to crouch in the silent heat, the adobe walls trembling in the haze. Across the roadway a piebald dog scratched its ribs, and off to the southern end, a windmill clattered listlessly as the warm wind blew tumbleweeds like fragments of forgotten dreams over the dirt.

Hawk unwound the reins from the hitching post and began to walk the big black horse around the cantina. As he entered the alleyway flanking the building he paused, listening.

There was the drumming of hooves on hard-packed sand, the reverberation like a heartbeat on the ground. He turned the horse, peering up the street as five riders cantered in. Automatically, he checked them. It was difficult to make out details through the shifting patterns of light and dust, but he saw that the group rode in a vee-shaped formation, almost military in their precision. At the head of the vee was a short, fat Mexican, a gigantic sombrero flashing conchos in the sunlight. He wore a sweat-stained yellow shirt that was crossed by twin bandoliers, all the loops filled with gleaming brass cartridges. His pudgy face was decorated with a flourishing mustache, the tips waxed so that they curled round like horns. He wore pearl-handled revolvers, cross-draw style, on both hips, and his pants were decorated down the sides with conchos that matched the display on his hat.

A few feet behind him there was another Mexican, tall and slender. Despite the heat, he wore a silver-threaded jacket that ended just above the silver-studded gunbelt spanning his narrow waist. His tight pants flared below the knees, revealing an inlay of more silver that flickered in the light, mingling with the reflections coming off his saddle and stirrups.

Hawk watched as they rode up to the cantina and dismounted, studying the three men last in line. They looked to be Americans, two wearing faded denim shirts with dark patches of sweat on the chests and sides; the third had a maroon shirt, the chest crossed by the thin band of a shoulder holster. The first two both wore standard holsters, tied down on their right thighs. Hawk recognized the familiar curve of Colt butts, and on the maroon-shirted man, the distinctive angle of a Smith & Wesson Schofield.

When they dismounted, the short Mexican took off his sombrero, revealing a shiny skull totally devoid of hair. He wiped a bandanna over the glistening skin and set the wide-brimmed hat back on his head. Beside him, the man in the maroon shirt tugged on a black frock-coat, adjusting the hang so that it covered the Schofield belted under his left arm.

All five removed their Winchesters from the saddle boots before entering the cantina.

Hawk frowned, trying to place their faces against his memories of wanted posters. No recollections came up, so he eased back into the alley and led the black horse down to the stable.

It was little more than a shed, the walls open on two sides and all the stalls facing in towards a central trough that was filled with murky water. He put the black in the shadiest pen and forked hay into the manger built against the interior wall. Then he unsaddled the animal and rubbed it down. When he was finished, he carried his gear to the room and dumped his saddle on the floor. The room was a hut, adobe walls with a palmetto roof that was thick with cobwebs and dark blots of spiders. There was a narrow bed with dirty sheets covering a stained mattress and a bolster that smelled faintly of whisky and vomit. A single window let light inside the room, filtering through the dust patterns on the glass. The door had a bolt on the inside.

Hawk lifted the mattress and watched the bugs run away, then he fetched the money from his saddlebags and spread it over the leather bindings that formed the base of the bed. Dropped the mattress back in place, and went out to the bath-house.

The barkeep had already filled the tub and there were three flies struggling to survive in the steaming water. Hawk flipped them clear and stripped off. He hung his gunbelt over his clothes, the butt of the Colt within easy reach, and set the Meteor on the dirt floor beside the tub.

He climbed into the water, hunching his knees to accommodate his height to the narrow confines of the vessel, and began to scrub the trail dirt from his body. When the water got grey he shaved and then climbed naked on to the ground. The barkeep had left two pails of cold water alongside: Hawk used them both to sluice the slime of soap from his body, then towelled dry.

As he got dressed the stormheads he had seen building let loose a single peel of thunder. It echoed like a faraway cannon, and for a brief instant the sky shone silver, then was abruptly dark. A few droplets of rain plopped lazily into the dust, producing miniature craters, like bullet holes in the earth. Hawk went back to the room and tilted the whisky bottle to his mouth. The light was starting to fade as the clouds drifted closer, and he checked over his guns with the door open. From inside the cantina he could hear the five men shouting and laughing.

He emptied the guns one at a time, cleaning the bores and the chambers before applying a little oil and reloading. He wiped a rag over the gunbelt and greased the inside of each holster. Then, when he was satisfied, he buckled the rig on his waist and slid the Colt and the Meteor loose a few times until he was confident of being able to draw as fast as he was able.

Then he went back to the cantina.

The place was filling up now, the tables getting occupied by drinkers and card players. The barkeep had lit some kerosene lanterns that were spreading pale yellow light through the room. It shone off the bleached hair of the two women drifting amongst the tables, sparking flutters of tawdry brilliance from the cheap jewellery they wore and the diamante decorations of their skimpy dresses. The men Hawk had seen coming in were clustered around a single table with a deck of cards passing amongst them.

Hawk went up to the bar and asked for a beer and some food. The barkeep opened his mouth to reply, but just then a massive blast of thunder shook the entire building. The lanterns hanging from the ceiling danced on their stanchions, sending wandering rays of light like multiple kaleidoscopes around the walls and floor. The bottles on the shelf behind the bar trembled, and Hawk felt the floor shake beneath his feet.

"Christ!" said the barkeep. "We got a big one comin'."

Then the rain got started in earnest. It hit like a Gatling gun, rattling a volley of water off the roof, splashing on to the street so that clouds of dust got lifted up and blown inside before the deluge quelled the rising and reduced the length of the main street to a watery sludge. A woman squealed, clutching the nearest man in mock terror, and the barkeep went over to the front and stepped out on to the porch. He unlatched the storm shutters and swung the wooden sections closed, then came back inside to fasten the frames. His apron and shirt were dark with moisture.

"Them ponies gonna get awful wet," he said. "You gents want to put 'em in the stable?"

The fat Mexican put down his cards and shook his head, grinning to expose a row of large, white teeth.

"They are used to living rough." He spoke almost perfect American, only the slurred *r* giving him away. "Like us."

The barkeep shrugged and the others laughed. Hawk lifted his mug, not interested.

"Goddam drifters." The barkeep poured himself a glass of whisky. "Don't make no sense to leave an animal out in weather like this. Not unless you're plannin' a fast getaway."

Hawk shrugged and sipped his beer.

"Ain't no reason, either," the barkeep went on, choosing Hawk as his listener on the basis that one gunman was better than five; especially if he was American. "No reason to want a fast getaway from here. We don't have no bank or stage office, nor no peace officer. No reason at all."

"Maybe we got our own reasons."

Hawk had seen the tall Mexican coming up to the bar. He had eased sideways so that his left elbow rested on the plank counter close to the pistol grip of the Meteor. His right hung by his side, close to the butt of the Colt.

"Maybe we got our own reasons that we don't like to talk about." His accent was more slurred than the fat man's, the consonants blurring and the *r*'s rolling thickly. "An' maybe we don't like other people discussing them."

Hawk could smell the liquor on his breath as he spoke. Knew that the empty bottle of whisky he was holding was far from the first drink he had taken. He shrugged.

"Your business, friend."

"I ain't yore friend," said the Mexican, setting the bottle on the bar. "I don't have no friends except my brother there, an' our *compadres*."

Hawk shrugged again, not wanting to get into a fight with a man who had four friends backing him. Not wanting to waste lead on a man with no bounty posted.

"Your problem," he said. "Mine is finding someplace quiet to eat."

From the rear of the room, one of the

Americans called, "Federico! Leave it. Ain't worth the trouble."

The Mexican turned, glancing at his brother. The fat man smiled, stroking a finger against the up-curve of his mustaches. The slim one turned back to face Hawk.

"You think we're too noisy, *gringo*?" He stepped clear of the bar, his thin-lipped mouth set in a sneer. "I guess you *yanqui pistoleros* don't have the *cojones* to enjoy yourselves properly."

Hawk's eyes got very cold. He set his mug down and shifted his weight on to both feet, balancing. He looked at the Mexican, and his voice came out cold and mean as his eyes.

"I got no quarrel with you, Mex. But if you're lookin' for a fight I hope you carry coin enough to pay the undertaker."

"I think you better take that back, *gringo*." The man's voice lost its laughter, the sneering fading under the wash of anger. "I don't like to be called that."

Hawk grinned. There was no humour in the expression. The man had come

19

looking for a fight and now he was primed up exactly as Hawk wanted: the insult of the "Mex" pushing him beyond that fine point where reason would dictate his actions, leaving only the irrational spur of rage.

"Sorry," he said, still smiling the ugly grin. "I never knew you greasers were so touchy."

"You don't know who I am?" The Mexican's lips trembled with fury, their movement matching the drumming of the rain on the roof. "You don't know Federico Brava?"

Hawk sniffed. There was a coldness inside him that superseded the danger of chancing a fight with five-on-one odds. He didn't like being pushed around. Didn't like getting talked into a fight that was not of his own making. Liked even less the idea of backing down.

It was like Hickok had told him once: "Man prods you, you got two choices. You face up or you crawl away. Crawlin' makes you dirty."

"I never heard of you," he said. "But

you greasers are mostly alike. It's hard to tell one bean puncher from another."

Federico Brava snarled, spittle flecking his lips. Hawk went on grinning, knowing that the prodding had tilted the balance in his favour. Take Federico with the first bullet, he thought, then go down firing on the others. He hoped the barkeep had a scattergun hidden under the counter. Hoped the man would use it.

"You got a choice," he said. "Walk away, or draw."

"*Bastardo!*"

Federico's hand dropped as he spat the insult. In the instant of clarity that slows violent action to a timeless void, Hawk saw that his fingers were carefully mani-cured, the nails clean, trimmed neatly. Then they were lost as the Mexican's hand fisted his gun, the slim fingers wrapping around the butt of the Colt's .45 Cavalry model.

Time stopped and speeded simul-taneously. Hawk's right hand closed on the wood grips of the Frontier model as his knees bent and he let himself fall backwards, pushing away from the bar. He saw the Colt begin to lift clear of Federico's holster as his own thumb closed down on the hammer of the Frontier model, his forefinger sliding with practised ease through the trigger guard. The gun was cocked as it cleared the polished leather, the muzzle lifting to point on the Mexican's belly while Federico's longer barrel was still hampered by the ornate holster.

He lifted his thumb, feeling rather than hearing the familiar thunder of the detonation.

For a moment that lasted just long enough for his shoulders to hit the floor, his vision was obscured by the cloud of the black powder smoke, the lightning flash that burst from the barrel.

Federico screamed and went back like a giant hand was dragging on his belt. His arms flew wide as though to allow more space for the red hole that blossomed on his belly, just above the silver buckle of his belt. Like an obscene rose that opened its petals and gave off the sudden stink of death. His Colt blasted a single shot into the ceiling, releasing a thin down-pouring of dust and three crushed spiders. He hit the floor and rolled over, spitting blood. The silver patterning that covered the back of his fancy jacket was abruptly dark, thick gouts of blood pulsing from the centre of a fist-sized hole that was sited a foot higher than his belt and just to the right of his spine. He dropped his Colt and pressed both hands against his stomach. The manicured nails got dirty with his dying, the ends cracking as they caught on the threading of his jacket and broke as he tried to hold his life inside him.

Hawk rolled, lifting up on his feet with the pistol cocked and pointing at the other four.

From the corner of his eye he saw the barkeep level a twin-barrelled Remington over the counter. The double hammers made a loud sound that somehow penetrated through the high-pitched squealing of the dying man. It was the loudest sound, for the cantina was suddenly still. Empty of any movement other than Hawk's.

He reached the table where the men were playing cards while the fat Mexican was still climbing to his feet. He had both hands crossed over his belly to clutch the grips of the pearl-handled revolvers. Two of the Americans were rising to their feet. One was hauling a Colt's Peacemaker from the holster, the other gaping at Hawk's speed as he fumbled for the revolver sheathed on his hip. Only the man in the black suit and maroon shirt was still seated. He was smiling.

Hawk set his left hand down on the table and spilled it over. Cards fluttered like confetti through the smoky air, the grease-stained faces contrasting with the brighter glint of falling money. The table slammed hard against the Mexican's wrists, tipping him off balance so that he careened into the man beside him, knocking the American's gun out of line.

Hawk levelled the Colt on the Mexican's face and said, "Leave it."

Behind him, too close for comfort, the

barkeep said: "No trouble! That was a fair fight." His voice was shaky with fear, but the Remington stayed pointed into the room. "The Mex pushed it too far. Everyone saw that, so you fellers just pick him up an' get him outta here."

Slowly, like angry snakes retreating back under their rocks, the pistols descended into the holsters. The man in the black coat stood up, a cold smile decorating his face. Hawk eased to the side, clear of the shotgun's blast.

"Let's go, Luis," said the American. "No point to pushin' it."

Hawk drew the Meteor left-handed. Cocked the ugly gun and only then dropped the Colt into the holster. He transferred the shotgun to his right hand, holding the cut-down barrel tight on the group of men as they shifted clear of the spilled table.

The fat Mexican went on staring at him, dark eyes liquid with suppressed rage. The rain went on drumming against the roof. Federico went on screaming, though now the sounds were fainter, getting throaty.

"You heard the man," snarled Hawk. "Get the crow-bait outta here."

The American in the black suit pulled on a pair of black gloves. He was careful to keep both hands in clear sight.

"Sure." His voice was dry, faintly tinged with a Southern accent; almost amused. "Just like you say."

"Cole?" The American who had drawn first spoke. "We just gonna walk away?"

"Don't know another thing to do against two scatterguns." The black-suited man stepped towards Federico. "Except maybe die."

"Jesus!" The other American spat. "That goes down hard."

"Not so hard as shot," grunted Hawk. "Do it."

All four men moved towards the dying Mexican. Federico began to scream afresh as they picked him up. The holes in his body left long streamers of blood on the fresh-scrubbed floor. Hawk backed against the bar as they went past, waiting until they reached the door before stepping out to the centre of the room with the

Meteor angled at the rectangle of darkness that was the opening to the rain-washed street.

The fat Mexican paused in the doorway, twisting his head to stare back at the gunfighter.

"He's my brother," he said quietly.

"I hope he ain't heavy," rasped Hawk. "But the ground should be soft enough for easy digging."

"My name is Luis Brava," said the Mexican. "Remember that. I want you to know my name when I kill you."

"Jared Hawk," said the gunfighter. "Compliment's returned."

The batwings swung shut, letting in a blast of rain. Hawk moved sideways to the door, staring out into the gloom past the screen of the frame. A small crowd had gathered, parting as the four men dumped Federico on his horse and tugged oil-skins over their clothes. Two of the Americans sided the Mexican, holding him upright in the saddle as the rain began to wash the blood clear of his belly and back. He went on moaning as they led the horse away to the north.

Luis paused a moment, spitting on to the porch.

"Luis Brava, *gringo*. You remember that."

"Shit!" Hawk dropped the Meteor back inside the holster. "Next thing, we'll be playing forget-me-not."

2

"**W**HAT you gonna do now?"
Hawk frowned. "Finish my
drink. Get somethin' to eat.
Sleep."

The barkeep shook his head. "You ain't
worried about them fellers comin' back?"

"No." Hawk poured whisky. "They
backed down when they had the chance to
kill me. They didn't take it—they won't
come back."

"Maybe they'll lay up fer you," said the
barkeep. "Ambush you someplace."

Hawk shrugged. "People tried that
before. Most like will again. I ain't about
to lose no sleep worrying on it."

"Jesus!" The barkeep shook his head
some more and set about serving the men
who had wandered in on the tail-end of
the fight, anxious to catch a look at the
hardman who had faced out five *pistoleros*.
Hawk could hear him whispering as he

filled the glasses. "Fastest goddam draw I ever saw . . . Mex was down an' dyin' while the others was still reachin' . . . Had 'em covered already." His voice got louder as he added, "O' course, I was coverin' 'em, too. Got both barrels pointed at 'em . . . Mighta been different, else."

Hawk picked up the bottle and pushed through the thin crowd. The rain was keeping most of the cantina's custom away, and had also served to deaden the sound of the shots. The few people watching him were those in the immediate vicinity of the cantina; storekeepers with little else to do except watch the downpour clear the dust from their windows and bemoan the loss of trade.

The storm was drifting south, following the line of the Rio Grande down into Mexico, and the worst part of the thunder was gone on the high altitude winds. It sounded like distant cannons now, cannons in the rain, leaving behind the aftermath of the clouds: a steady, relentless drive of rain that curtained the street in grey and chilled the previously-warm air. Hawk estimated that it would be fully clear by midnight, and that by dawn the ground would be baking solid again. He sat down at the table he had occupied before.

The barkeep came over: "Food?"

"That's what I said." Hawk ignored the curious stares directed his way. He was accustomed to them by now; ignored them. "And soon."

"You bet." The barkeep nodded. "It'll be on the house. We ain't had this much excitement in a twelvemonth."

"I guess," said Hawk. "Thanks for backing me."

"Weren't nothin'." The barkeep swelled visibly, puffing out his chest and wiping the cowlick from his forehead. "Do the same again."

Hawk nodded and said, "Next time get up the end of the bar. That way the next ones'll need to turn two ways."

"Oh, Christ!" The florid face went pale. "I never thought of that."

"Keeps you alive," said Hawk. "Thinking like that."

The man nodded, swallowing hard. He disappeared through a side door, emerging a while later with two plates. One was piled high with chili, the other with biscuits. Hawk began to eat.

The rain went on falling and the conversation around the bar went on growing as more people drifted in as the evening got older. Hawk concentrated on his food, taking no notice of the pointing fingers or the whispered comments. He emptied half the bottle and then stood up. Went to the bar.

"How much?"

"Like I said." The barkeep smiled, glancing round to check that everyone could hear him. "It's on the house. On account of how we worked together back there."

"Thanks." Hawk grinned, not averse to collecting a free meal. "Thanks a lot."

"Nothin'." The barkeep preened. "My pleasure."

Hawk nodded and went out the door to the alley.

The rain was still coming down, but

now it was settled into a thinner spill, deflecting off the gutters so that the areas closest to the walls were relatively dry. He reached his room and cursed as he saw a pool spreading over the floor, filled by the steady spout that came in through a hole in the roof. The bed was dry, not quite far enough over to catch the leak. He lifted the mattress, checking that his money was still in place, then stripped off and climbed under the sour sheets. The Colt was resting under his pillow; the scattergun beside him, under the blanket.

Sleep came fast.

Dawn and an early rising cock woke him. The light filtered in through the dirty window and the edges of the door. Where the rain had come in, there was now a single, thin ray of sun. The cock crowed, its stridency sending thin tendrils of pain through his skull: he realized that he had drunk too much, and damned his foolishness.

Then he grinned, telling himself to forget it. It had been a long time since he relaxed. The ride down to Terra Alta had occupied the better part of a month, and during that time he had drunk nothing, concentrating on the trail left by Benny Levitz and Berny Levy. When he had caught up with them, and killed them, the marshal in Terra Alta had made it pretty clear that he would appreciate Hawk's swift departure. The gunfighter had concurred: there was little point to angering a duly appointed peace officer who might be signing bounty notes in the future. Cabanos had been the first settlement he had seen since then, and he figured he had a little relaxation coming his way.

He got dressed and went out to the bath-house. The tub had got filled up during the night, so he dunked his head and shaved cold, leaving his collar-length black hair to dry on its own. Then went inside the cantina to find some breakfast.

He ate bacon and eggs with a mass of fried potato and a full pot of bitter black coffee. There was no one else in the saloon, so this time he had to pay. Then he went out and saddled his horse, pleased to find that the stable was built better than his room. He walked the black pony on to the main street and over to Cabanos's single general store. There he bought supplies for the journey northwards to Valverde; remounted, and rode away.

Cabanos was settled along a fold of land that was flanked on both sides by tall ridges. To the south, the country flattened out, the ridges spreading like a whore's legs to form a wide vee. To the north, in keeping with the general configuration, the land rose up into shadow, high hills exposing a single pass that led to where he wanted to go.

The ground was still damp, the early sun lifting a thin mist from the rain-soaked soil like sweat from a whore's thighs. Hawk rode straight up the main street, leaving the little town behind him as he began to climb the waterlogged slope fronting the pass. He rode easily, holding the black pony to a steady canter. His eyes, shaded from the sun by the black hat, moved steadily from side to side, checking the terrain ahead. Every so often he twisted in the saddle and scanned the downslope behind.

There was no sign of movement in any direction.

By mid-morning the ground was dried out, the moisture left by the storm evaporated under the fierce glare of the New Mexico sun. Up ahead, the pass got darker as the sun shifted to its zenith and began to angle across the hills to the west. Hawk reached it around noon and dismounted.

On either side, like the walls of a narrow alleyway, sheer rock tumbled down, colours blending into a confusion of black and red and yellow. The sun lit the upper reaches, shining bright gold along the rimrock, but at the bottom, where the trail passed through, there was only shadow.

He rested his horse, leaving it to crop the grass as he opened a can and forked beans and ham into his mouth. When he was finished, he scooped out a shallow hole and buried the can before mounting again and riding cautiously towards the mouth of the pass. He drew the Meteor as he approached the shadows, resting the ugly gun across his saddlehorn with his right hand cupped around the grip, thumb on the hammer and forefinger firm on the trigger.

It was quiet in the pass, the sound of the black horse's shod hooves ringing loud on the hard ground, echoing from the walls. Up ahead, he could make out the patch of light that marked the northern-most extension of the split. As he got closer, he heeled the pony to a canter, steering with left hand and knees; his right hand carried the scattergun pointed forwards by his side, angled over the pony's head.

The light got brighter and the exit got wider. He could already make out the land beyond, folds covered with piñon and cedar, aspens thick along the middle slopes, their leaves already beginning to turn gold as summer ended and fall approached. The pass spread out to the north, the walls sloping more gently, with rockfalls stumbling broken stone along both sides.

He emerged into sunlight, ducking his head as he gave his eyes time to adjust to the brightness, still keeping the horse to a canter, trusting it to pick its own way.

And a rope landed neatly over his shoulders, tugged tight by his own forwards motion.

It was expertly thrown, dropping to his elbows while he was still reacting to the movement, pinning both arms against his ribs. The shotgun blasted a pattern of useless shot against the sky as he felt himself lifted clear of the saddle. For a moment there was only the vacuum of descent, the pressure of the noose about his waist. Then he hit the ground with a thud that sent tremors of pain up through his spine into his mind. There was a wash of darkness that burst with bright, scattered light across the balls of his eyes, and nausea roiled in his gut, pain and whisky and greasy chili fighting together so that he gasped and began to choke. At the same time, he was twisting over and round, grinding his boots against the rock in an attempt to move back far enough towards the roper that he would gain leeway to wriggle the noose clear.

The hidden man was too good: as Hawk shifted back, he drew in the slack, keeping the lariat tight. Hawk grunted, slowing his movements. Then braced both feet and pushed himself back in a wild dive that ground sharp outlines of stone against his back.

As he landed, a second rope dropped about his ankles, the noose snapping taut as the pressure got taken up. Abruptly, he was stretched out, legs drawn stiff and arms secured firmly to his sides.

Luis Brava came out from behind a rock. He had changed his yellow shirt for a bright red blouse with billowing sleeves and a round collar. The wax that had held his mustache curled into place was spoiled by the rain, so that the tips drooped down on either side of his fleshy lips. He was smiling. It was not a pretty smile, nor at all friendly

Behind him, the American in the black

suit was grinning at Hawk, hands folded under his jacket.

"I told you we'd meet again," snarled Brava. "I told you I'd kill you."

Hawk said nothing, just concentrated on relaxing his arms enough that the rope wouldn't cut off the blood flow and deprive him of movement.

"You know how long it took Federico to die?" Brava stepped up close, lifting a foot to bring the heel of his boot down on Hawk's belly. "You know how long?"

Hawk winced as the metal-studded heel dug against the muscle. "I seen gutshots take up to thirty hours," he grunted. "Way I hit your *hermano*, I'd say he had three, no more."

Brava ground the heel deeper, setting all his weight behind the pressure. The smile left his face, lips curving down into a line that matched the droop of his mustache. Sweat beaded Hawk's forehead. He tried to brace his stomach muscle against the grinding of the boot.

"Five, *gringo*," said Brava. "Five hours

of pain. Most of that stinking night. That's how long he took to die."

"Tough," groaned the American. "I must've drunk too much."

"*Bastardo!*" Brava's foot left Hawk's stomach. It landed on the ground and swung back. Came forwards in a sweeping kick that ended along the side of the gunfighter's jaw. "*Bastardo!*"

Hawk turned his face as he saw the kick coming, trying to ride it. He succeeded in avoiding most of the force, but the pointy toe still caught the underside of his chin, and the sole rasped skin from his cheek. Fresh lights danced over his eyes and he felt his mouth fill with vomit.

He spat, fighting to clear his mouth and throat of the choking puke. It spattered over his lips, dribbling on to his shirt and vest. Brava kicked him some more, aiming the blows at his waist. Hawk writhed, doing what little he could to protect his ribs and kidneys. There wasn't very much, and after a while that seemed to last a lifetime he felt his eyes close and all the sickness in his gut come bursting up.

41

He coughed it out, tasting the rancid memories that spurted over his chest and flooded thickly over his vest. Somewhere deep inside him a little spark of determination burned. It was compounded of his natural instinct to survive and the raw hate he felt for Luis Brava, and it survived the kicking so that when that ended he could still—dimly—make out what the four men were saying.

His eyes were watering and his ears felt like waves were beating inside his skull. Very faintly, like figures in a bad dream, he saw the two denim-shirted Americans come up to look at him. They were coiling ropes, and as the coils got thicker he saw that they had unfastened his ankles and arms. They stood up and went over to join the two dim shapes a yard clear of his bruised body. One shape was short and squat, shadowed even further by the sombrero. The other was taller and darker. Hawk moaned and stretched his right hand down towards the Colt still holstered on his right side.

He got the pistol halfway clear of

the holster before anyone noticed. The hammer was cocked and his finger was fitting numbly through the trigger guard when a boot ground his wrist against the rock and someone stood on his legs. He screamed. And the world went away into a vortex of whirling red darkness that began in his mind and then spun deeper inside him until there was nothing else.

"Kill him now." The man in the black suit glanced at Hawk's supine body. "Put a bullet in his gut an' leave him fer the crows."

"No." Luis Brava shook his head. "That's too easy."

"What else we gonna do with him?" asked one of the others. "Bastard's half-way dead already."

"Exactly," said Brava. "So if I shoot him in the gut, he'll die fast."

"Christ!" The second American added his opinion. "Just leave him, then. We take his horse, he ain't overly likely to do nothin' but crawl away someplace to die."

"We don't need extra horses," snapped

Brava. "One will be enough, so we can take Federico's. Another just slows us down."

"So shoot it," said the man in the black suit. "Horse an' rider both."

"No." Brava sucked the drooping strands of his mustache into his mouth. "We keep them both alive. Put him on the horse."

"You're crazy, Luis!" said the man in the black suit. "What the goddam hell are you thinkin' about?"

Brava's face got pale, then red. He spat the strands of chewed hair from his lips and turned to face the taller man. His arms were crossed over his waist.

"It took Federico five hours to die, Cole. Five hours of pain. You *gringos* don't understand these things. This one must suffer as much. Longer."

The man called Cole shrugged. "You're the boss. Whatever you say. But we don't have five hours to waste watchin' him die."

"It don't matter," said Brava. "Just do like I tell you. Get him on his horse and bring Federico along, too."

The three Americans shrugged and hauled Hawk clear of the ground. They tried to avoid the vomit coating his chest and sides as they put him across the saddle of the black horse and lashed his hands and legs under the animal's belly. Then they took Federico's wrapped body and tied it in place on his pony.

"Down there," said Brava, pointing to the wide spread of hot sand at the foot of the hills. "Let's go."

Somewhere along the trail leading to the flatlands Hawk woke up. He was barely conscious, and then only aware of pain. His belly hurt where it was bounced against the hard leather of the saddle, and his head spun; his right arm felt like a wagon had rolled over it, and his ankles were numb.

He closed his eyes and began to swallow and yawn, trying to fight the sickness of the beating and the abrupt descent clear of his head. He wasn't very successful, and by the time they reached the low ground he felt only slightly better than his start. But he could hear what they said.

He recognized Luis Brava's voice.

"Here." The Mexican pointed at a wide sand-spill, this flanked by high walls of bare rock. "This will do."

Hawk felt the ropes around his feet cut loose; watched as a knife sliced through the bindings on his wrists and a boot lifted clear of a stirrup to shove his face up and over the saddle. He collapsed on to the ground, no longer able to feel the bruising of the fall.

"Cut enough pegs to stake out two men," said Luis Brava. "Do it fast."

It wasn't long before Hawk felt his arms and legs spread out in an x-shape. His body was spread between the four pegs, wrists and ankles lashed tight to the splinters of pine driven deep into the dry ground.

"Now put Federico out the same way," said Luis Brava. "Beside the *gringo*."

"Christ Jesus!" Hawk couldn't recognize the speaker. "I thought we was gonna bury him."

"No," said Luis. "This way it looks like Apaches done it, so we don't get no blame. Besides, there's another reason."

"What reason?" someone asked. "I don't get it."

"That's why I'm the *jefe*," said Brava, "an' you do like you're told."

Time passed. The sun shifted across the sky. Ants crawled over Hawk's body and each thud of the four pins going into the ground around Federico's body sent tremors up through the gunfighter's ribs to coalesce into shimmering waves of pain inside his head.

Then Luis spilled water over his face. Turned to Hawk and asked, "You want some?"

Hawk didn't answer. He didn't want to, and he couldn't: his lips were slimed with vomit and his mouth was dry, too arid to secrete the saliva necessary for words. Luis upended the canteen anyway, splashing water over Hawk's face and then kneeling down to dribble the liquid into the gunfighter's mouth.

Without wanting to, Hawk swallowed.

47

The water was warm and tasted faintly of tequila and fur, but it refreshed him. He opened his eyes, staring up at Brava.

"Good," said the Mexican, "that's very good. *Muy bueno.* I want you to live a long time, *hombre.*"

"I thought you wanted to kill me." It was difficult to get the words out. "I thought you were spittin' on my grave."

"I am," said Brava; laughing. "You shot Federico in the gut yesterday. He's been dead around fifteen hours. He's starting to smell. Come nightfall, there's gonna be coyotes an' wolves pick up the scent. In the morning, the vultures will see. Then they start to come down. Pretty soon, they pick over what the dogs left an' still feel hungry. They turn to you."

He stood up; chuckling.

"I reckon it's gonna take them a while to pick through that fancy vest. But then they'll be dipping their beaks inside your belly. And all that time you're gonna be stretched out alongside Federico, knowing that he's the reason they're plucking yore

48

guts. You think about that, *mister Jared Hawk*." He spat, landing the gobbet on Hawk's face so that it dripped slowly off the battered cheek into the mouth. "You think about that while you get very slowly killed."

Hawk watched him walk away. Watched him come back with the black pony. Saw his gunbelt draped over the saddle. Brava looped the reins around the pine pin holding Hawk's left foot to the ground and chuckled some more. He opened Hawk's canteen and checked the water. Filled it. Then hung it on the saddlehorn.

"Storm's gone," he said. "Tomorrow'll be hotter than today. You'll get thirsty. When you do, you look at that horse and think about the water. Think about how you could ride it away from here. If you weren't tied down with wolves an' coyotes an' vultures tearing out your guts. When you think of that, you take a look at Federico. They'll take him first, because he's already dead. You, Jared Hawk, you've got a whole lot of suffering to go."

Hawk closed his eyes and listened to the hoofbeats fading away over the hard, dry folds of the wide valley. For a spell, he lay against the sand, relaxing long enough for the riders to be gone. It was already close on sunset, the eastern edge of the bowl beginning to fade away into shadowy lines where the dying sun got filtered through the trees and clefts of the western slopes.

When all the sounds of movement had got lost through the pine thickets covering the lower ridges he twisted his head to examine the body beside him.

Federico Brava was naked. His belly was covered with a fan of blood that mingled with the hair covering his lower belly and groin. His clothes—the fancy, silver-threaded suit, the gunbelt, his boots —were folded neatly beside him. Over his body there crawled a triple line of ants. One column was scouring the hole, a second carrying whatever bounty it had found away. The third was investigating the mouth.

High up in the sky, like exclamation marks against the darkening blue, like undertakers awaiting their prey, a spiral of vultures circled down.

Off to the south, high up, where the rimrock curved over into the next fold of the Rio Grande country, a lobo howled. The cry was answered by others, the baying joining together so that Hawk couldn't tell how many there were.

The sound almost drowned out the higher-pitched yowling of the coyotes to the south and west. Theirs was much closer, nearer than the long distance sound of the wolves.

Hawk watched the sun go down, fading away behind the western ridge. Watched the column of vultures settle over the crags around his position; and listened to the coyotes move closer.

He tugged at the cords holding his wrists and ankles to the pins; hoping to drag a rope—or peg—free.

Nothing came loose, and all his efforts

brought was more pain, lancing up through his limbs and belly in sharp spurts of fire; hot and heavy waves that closed his eyes as nausea roiled sickly through his gut.

Sometime during the night he woke up to the sound of music. But when he opened his eyes, he saw that the timpani was the clash of bones against teeth, the strumming coming from the pipes and tubes the coyotes were dragging loose from Federico's body.

He tried to shout at the grey-flanked predators, but only red and yellow eyes answered his protest: the teeth went on moving.

He woke again because the sound was gone. Opened his eyes into two enormous red orbs that seemed to give off a gusting exhalation of foul breath, like the stink of a corpse. Like Federico Brava.

He shouted. And the coyote that had been standing on his chest, ready to rip out his throat, yelped once and ran away.

Its passage took the others clear of Federico Brava's corpse. Hawk turned his head to study the animals' work. Then gagged and turned away, fighting the cords pinning his body to the ground, where it might be dealt with the same way as the Mexican's.

Federico Brava no longer looked like a human being. His belly was open, most of the skin and flesh ripped loose from the ribcage so that the white lines of the few ribs left unchewed were sticking up through an ugly curtain of tattered flesh. A long spill of entrails was torn clear of his buttocks, the glistening strands shining yellow and blue under the moon's pale light. Ants, like thin runnels of blood, formed dark passages over the sides; out from the empty sockets of the eyes; from the gaping hole of the mouth.

"No," Hawk said. "Not me. I'm not dead. Not yet."

He fought against the ropes holding him to the ground where the coyotes and the vultures could tear his life away and refused to accept the inevitability of death.

"No!" he shouted. "That chilly wind don't blow. Not yet."

3

FOR the rest of the night he stayed awake, shouting each time the coyotes came close. His hoarse yelling drove the grey-flanked animals clear of his position, but there was no way he could drive them from Federico Brava's corpse. He watched it reduced to a bloody ruin that, by the time the sun came up and began to fill the bowl with heat, was little more than the mangled outline of a man.

The black horse helped him stay awake, screaming as the coyotes drifted in and kicking out at the predators as they sought to sneak beneath the lashing hooves to sink their fangs into the soft underflesh of the belly. The horse's animosity kept them away from it and Hawk, but the furious attempts to drag loose the retaining rein failed to shift the peg. Hawk groaned as the first rays of the early sun struck his face: he had hoped the pony would tear the peg clear so that he might gain sufficient leeway to work his other bonds loose. But Brava had driven the pin too deep: it remained firm.

The sun came up and the bowl of rock-encrusted sand got hot. The sky shifted from the pearly grey of the pre-dawn to the roseate hues of a bright new day. Then the opalescent tint faded from the sky, replaced by the hot blue of a pure New Mexico sky. The coyotes faded away and Hawk watched the vultures spiral like black omens above the sand. Ants crawled across his face, and for longer than he liked to think about, a scorpion scuttled over his chest, investigating the streamers of vomit coating his body. He closed his eyes to shut out the brilliance and the horror, concentrating on breathing slowly and relaxing so that his body gave up as few of its fluids as was possible.

He opened them again when he heard the heavy beating of wings close by him, and the thud of an ungainly body landing beside him.

The vulture was around two feet high,

its scraggy wings spreading shade over his face as it fanned air in an attempt to catch its balance. A rufflet of greyish feathers surrounded the serpentine, naked neck, then a smaller circlet of dull red plumes. The head appeared bald, skull-like, with dark, blank eyes examining his chest and belly from above a hooked, yellow beak. Like bleached bone.

Hawk opened his mouth to shout, but all that came out was a dry rasping sound that got lost under the clacking of the beak. The vulture craned its neck around as three more birds landed and began to waddle cumbrously over the sand. The first carrion bird let loose a croaking cry, and the others flapped awkwardly around Hawk's body to clamber on to Federico's. They seemed to chuckle as they studied the wounds opened by the coyotes, then sank their ugly heads deep inside the open ribcage.

The beaks came out dripping, with sticky streamers of glistening fat and thinner tubes of intestine getting gulped down the curving throats.

The first bird—the largest—hawked a cry of triumph into the burning air and hopped on to the gunfighter's legs. Hawk winced as the talons gripped his thigh, and jerked his body upwards and sideways.

The vulture squawked, beating its wings to maintain its balance, struggling back from the source of the unexpected sound.

The black horse squealed and began to buck again. And the vulture, surprised by the sudden extra sound, stumbled loose from Hawk's legs and tried to gain purchase on the sky. A hoof landed on a wing, thudding down over the fragile hollow bones The vulture let out a strident shriek and twisted its head to peck at the larger animal's plunging hooves. The horse chose to focus its panic and its fury on the nearest target. The vulture's left wing got trapped under a hoof, blood flecking the grubby black pinions. It twisted, snapping its yellow-bone beak at the fetlocks. The horse squealed its annoyance and thudded both forefeet against the bird's chest. The delicate ribcage shattered. Blood pulsed thinly over the hooves, and the bird's head flopped back, a red-black tongue protruding from the under-side of the beak. The horse went on stamping until there was nothing left except a thin spread of broken flesh with two wings and two scrawny legs that matched the bald neck.

The other birds took flight, panicked by the unexpected attack from easy prey.

And the day went on.

It was hot. Hawk felt his face blister. Felt his lips get dry and begin to crack. He kept his eyes closed, fearful that he might go blind under the hot sun, and after a while stopped listening for the sounds of danger and let the tempting arms of sleep snatch him away.

Cool night air woke him and he opened his hurting eyes on the pale silver face of the moon. The night was quiet of the sounds a rider might hear, and horribly loud with the noises a man facing death could listen to. Bats fluttered overhead, and off to the south a badger snuffled through the undergrowth. The wolves were howling again, and the coyotes were slinking closer. As Hawk listened, he heard a ferret dart across the hollow.

And then the coyotes moved in again.

It was hard to spot them because his eyes were as weary as his body and he found it hard to focus exactly on the slinking shapes. He wondered if Luis Brava was going to be successful in his choice of revenge. Wondered what a trickle of water might taste like. Wondered what it felt like to die.

Then something tugged at his ankle.

He forced his head up and forced his eyes to focus. Saw a coyote chewing on the corpse of the dead vulture. The black pony was too weary to protest, too exhausted by the heat and the fighting to do anything but stand with its head down and leave the scavenger dog free to chew its fill.

Two more slunk in, squabbling over the remains. Then began to gnaw on the splashed remnants of the vulture's life.

Hawk felt sharp teeth snap against his boot. His left boot. Close to the peg securing the black horse: the one covered thickly with the vulture's blood. He turned his head, and saw that the bindings holding him to the ground were made of plaited rawhide. Oiled leather.

And the fastenings around his left ankle were soaked in blood.

He felt them part as the coyotes chewed on the succulent material, and swung his leg free, landing the sole of his boot against a surprised snout.

The coyote yelped and sprang back, lips curling from yellow teeth. The others barked, slinking into the moonlit shadow with fangs bared and low, angry growls roiling up from inside their chests.

The additional threat panicked the black horse, sending it back in a flailing wave of hooves and snapping teeth. Hawk felt his left leg yanked up with agonizing force. Felt his whole body shifted sideways, so that his ribs and chest and arms got stretched out inside a curtain of pain that ran up through his shoulders into his head.

But the single cold fact remained, the

hard fact: Luis Brava had fixed the reins around the peg and his ankle, both.

It burned in his mind, overcoming the pain and the thirst and the beating: he had a chance to survive. A chance to cheat the predators of their prey and go on to find the men who had left him to die. A chance to take the vengeance he saw as his right. To even the score. To kill them.

It gave him the strength he needed.

He shouted at the coyotes, already scurrying clear of the unexpected activity, frightened by the plunging horse, and then spoke quietly to the pony.

It was difficult, because his mouth was parched and the words came out in a low, throaty grumble of indistinct sound. But the horse calmed, ceasing its nervous stamping and ducking its head as he spoke to it. It began to come closer, head down. Close enough that he was able to ram his free foot against its mouth and send it prancing back with the reins dragging tight around his left ankle.

He screamed as the animal's backwards movement yanked against his leg. Then his screaming became mingled with joy as he felt the pegs holding his wrists tear loose from the sand, dried and cracked now by the alternation of rain and heat. He doubled over, wrapping both hands around the single remaining peg. Dragged it loose from the ground as the horse stamped back and hauled him yards clear of the bodies marking his grave.

He hurt. Hurt badly, with needles of fire flashing along the nerve endings of his arms and shoulders and back and legs. There was no longer any feeling in his left leg, only a screaming banshee of agony in his hip. He thought it was dislocated, and when he got the reins free of his ankle and tried to stand up, he fell down. He kept the reins tight in both hands, and after a while the pain subsided to a numbing ache that brought fresh spills of hollow vomit from his empty stomach.

For some time the dry retching held him stretched on the ground as surely as the pegs. Then he rolled on to his back and eased the horse slowly closer, until he could reach up far enough to unhook the canteen from the saddle and take a long, long swallow.

The water was warm. It tasted of heat and death and life. He drank again and set the waterbottle to the side, reaching over to fasten the reins about the black pony's forefeet.

When he was certain the animal was hobbled firm he reached down to check his legs. His wrists were bloody where the rawhide had cut into the flesh as the pegs were hauled loose, and his right ankle was bruised even through the protection of his boot. His left leg was dislocated at the hip: he could feel the knob of bone jutting against the material of his pants, threatening to burst out through the flesh.

He plucked a shell from his gunbelt and stuck it between his teeth. Bit hard on the cold brass and rammed both hands down over the knob of his damaged thigh.

His scream was dampened by the bullet, and he thought his teeth would shatter as he bit down, but the hip joint snapped back in place. He fell back, sweat beading his face, running down into the dark hair and the stubble on his cheeks.

When he opened his eyes again the moon was passed over the sand, shining bright and cold as his hate against the western rockface and the exist passage beyond. The exit to the north, where Luis Brava and the others had gone.

He unwound the reins from the black pony's forefeet and wrapped them about his left wrist. Then he dragged the horse's head down and fastened an arm over its neck. It took him a long time, but he finally managed to climb on to the saddle. He hurt. Hurt badly, all through his body, and the cool wind that blew up from the slope in front of him lifted sour memories of vomit against his nostrils and mouth. He urged the pony forwards, letting it choose its own pace and its own path; so long as it headed northwards, along the trail he thought Brava and his men had taken.

"Ain't it funny," he mumbled, more to keep up his spirits than for any other reason, "how dead men make so much trouble. I never chose that fight, but now I'm coming to kill you. Funny how life can be."

4

BY the time the sun rose he was clear of the rocks, traversing a grassy slope that was bordered on its northern perimeter by thick stands of cottonwoods. He was moving slowly, letting the black horse walk despite his impatience. Any faster pace sent tremors of pain running through his body, threatening to blank out his vision under the assault of nausea, and he was afraid of toppling from the pony. The reins were tied about his left wrist, around the cuff of the black glove. The beating, the lack of food, the exposure, most of all the savage punishment he had taken breaking free, had weakened him badly. He realized that he would have to stop at some point, if only to rest the horse, but until that time came he wanted to cover as much ground as possible, rest as much as he was able in the saddle.

He was guessing that Brava and his men had come this way, basing the assumption on his knowledge of the terrain and memories of the few maps he had seen on the ride up from Terra Alta. Valverde was about a week's ride distant—for a healthy man travelling at a reasonable pace. The way Hawk was moving, the town might have been the other side of the Missouri, but in between he recalled noting a couple of smaller settlements. One was a place called Green Springs; the other, Cadillo. He couldn't remember how far they were from Cabanos, nor which came first, but he thought the Mexican and his American sidekicks must be heading for one of them. There wasn't much else around, except rugged country and mountain meadows and Apaches. He hoped he didn't run into any Indians: too many wanted to lift his hair.

The sun climbed up over the rimrock and began to heat the slope. The sunburn on his face began to sting, the blisters cracking and peeling so that the runnels of salty sweat coursing down his forehead and cheeks maintained a constant prickling that added a further dimension to his general discomfort. He ignored the aches, steering the pony towards the cottonwoods, where the timber offered shelter from the storm of heat.

Inside the trees the air was cool and still. It was very quiet, the light dim with only a few slanting rays of sunlight breaking through the thick overlay of foliage. The trail led in a straight line northwards, traversing the flank of the Jornado del Muerto range with the Rio Grande somewhere off to the west. It was some time later that he saw the light get brighter as the trees thinned out, and glanced up to find the sun directly overhead. His leg was throbbing, the hip swollen and hot. He knew that it needed some kind of cold compress to reduce the internal bruising, but until he found a ready supply of water he was wary of using his canteen.

He urged the horse on through the trees, emerging on a second grassy slope that curved in a wide crescent shape around a spur of the mountains. The rock climbed up several hundred feet above him, ending in a sharp wedge that jutted out on to the grass. It was broken at the foot, piled up in a series of massive slabs like gigantic playing cards frozen in the act of falling. The black horse pricked up its ears and let out a weary snicker as they approached the rocks, its pace quickening so that Hawk's leg was jarred, hot waves of agony darting up and down his body. He dragged on the reins, but the animal fought the pressure of the bit, struggling to move faster. Hawk groaned and allowed it to gather speed.

They crossed the grassland and came into the area of shadow formed by the landslip. The horse slowed as its hooves transferred from the grass to stone, and from up ahead, the man caught the sound of what the animal had smelled: water. He loosed the reins, allowing the pony to choose its own pace, then grunted with pleasure as they rounded a tall fold of broken rock.

Directly before him was a shallow depression, a triangular shape with high walls on two sides. The third side of the triangle was a steep, shale-covered slope that ran down a mile or more before a tree-thick terrace ended the slide. The bottom of the depression was covered with rich grass where soil had gathered. Across the centre, descending from a point midway up the apex of the walls and disappearing over the edge of the drop, was a stream.

The horse trotted up to the water and dropped its head. Hawk dragged his left foot from the stirrup, using both hands to attain the necessary leverage, then swung his good leg clear and over. He managed to get his right foot down first, but even so there was a moment of pure agony as he set his damaged leg down. He clutched the saddlehorn, gritting his teeth. Then, still leaning against the horse, he removed his gunbelt and tossed it over to the bank. After that he eased cautiously down until he could unwind the reins from his wrist and lash them about the pony's fetlocks. As an extra precaution, he fastened his rope to the saddlehorn, looping the other end about his waist: losing the horse now would be pure foolishness.

He went over to the stream, part crawling, part hopping. The water was clean and fast-flowing, shining silver in the sun as it gurgled over the rocks. It was about two feet deep, the banks spaced five feet apart. Hawk dragged his body into the water directly over his damaged leg.

His pants were quickly soaked through, his boots filling so that his toes numbed as the coolness of the mountain stream hit them. More importantly, the hot throbbing in his left hip began to subside. He sighed, reaching down to cup handfuls of water that he splashed over his burning face. It had seldom felt so good.

Across the stream, the horse began to crop the grass, snuffling its contentment. Hawk grinned. Then winced as the stretching of his facial muscles burst a blister, and closed his eyes.

He must have slept, for when he opened them again, the sun was shifted across the sky and his legs were beginning to sting with cold. He clambered awkwardly to his

71

feet, clothes cascading water as he stood up. His leg was still stiff, but he could put weight on it now without falling down, so he limped on to the grass and took the rope from his waist. There was a stubby spread of bushes growing to the east of the miniature canyon and he fastened the rope there. Then he stripped naked and examined his body.

His stomach and ribs bore the marks of Luis Brava's kicking, and the underside of his right wrist, halfway between elbow and hand, was an ugly purple colour. Both wrists were encircled by swollen red welts where the panicked horse had torn him free, but so far as he could tell, there was nothing broken. He was able to flex his fingers, and when he parodied a draw he felt sure his speed was only fractionally slowed.

He couldn't check his back or his face, though he could feel the swelling along his jawline, and the skin from the neck to the point was sore to his touch. Even so— given what he had been through—he was in surprisingly good shape.

He limped back to the stream and eased down into the cold water. It took his breath away now, but he stretched full length, ducking his head under the surface to let the cleansing liquid cover his entire body. He stayed there until he began to shiver, then climbed out and rolled on the grass like an animal before shifting to the sunniest patch and stretching out.

The afternoon was warm, and the angle of the rocks formed a natural trap for the sun. His body dried fast, but he remained supine, letting the heat sink into his hip and ease the bruises away as his clothes dried.

He waited until the sun was passed over to the west and the air was growing cooler before dressing again. Then he checked his guns and mounted the black horse. It was still difficult to climb into the saddle, and he knew that any kind of fast movement on foot was impossible, but the worst of the bruising appeared to be gone and in a few days he hoped to be fully limber.

And it would take a few days to reach the nearest town.

He turned the pony north and followed the trail around the outspill of rock, heading along the path he now felt certain Brava must have taken. When he grinned, the blisters no longer hurt.

Green Springs was seventy miles north of Hawk's position, maybe two days' ride for a fit man on a fresh horse. Given strength and a good pace, it was, at most, three days away from the bowl where Luis Brava had pegged the gunfighter out to die.

It was a small town, but wealthy. The main street was three hundred yards in length, the boundaries marked at one end by a clapboard church, and the other by the sheriff's office and the brick structure of the four-cell jail. In between there was a saloon with an adjoining hotel, an eating house, and a spread of stores. A stage office and a bank faced one another across the packed dirt of the road, the depot with a stable and corral built out behind. The road ran on a north-south axis, disappearing into a narrow pass two miles south of the town. The horns of rock forming the pass spread out just beyond into a small valley, rich with the natural springs that had given the place its name. The fan shape continued ten miles north-wards, then folded in again so that from above, the valley would have appeared like a diamond, or a teardrop.

Green Springs had been found back in the '50s by a wandering miner called Aloysius Stotter. He was convinced the Jornado del Muerto range must hold gold, and when people told him the country was too dangerous—that the Apache would kill him—he decided he had found the edge he had been looking for. Together with his partner, a slightly older man called Nathan Whitehead, and two mules, he went up into the Jornados and began to look around.

They got picked up by a mixed band of Chiricahua and Mimbreños before they found any gold, but when they swore they were only planning to dig out enough for their own needs without telling anyone else about the strike—if they made one—the Indians let them go. In part it was the pleading of a trader called Kieron Gunn that saved their lives. Gunn obviously had a lot of influence with the tribes, and it was he who extracted the promises from both sides.

Stotter and Whitehead went on to find a modest vein of gold. They dug out enough to see them through the winter in Doña Ana, and went back the next spring. They dug out some more—enough to set them both up for life—and decided to call it quits. Then they met a representative of the International Production Company of Philadelphia. He offered them almost as much as the year's labour had brought them for full rights in the strike— providing it still looked promising. Stotter and Whitehead forgot about their promise to Kieron Gunn and the Apaches, and led a party of IPC men into the Jornados.

The mineralogist declared that the vein was still fruitful, and the engineer said he could dig a deeper tunnel to the core of the shaft. The IPC man made out a cheque and they all headed back to Doña Ana. Along the way, they got jumped by

Mimbreños. Stotter, Whitehead, and three others were killed. The IPC man and two mule packers escaped.

By then, Fort McRae was built up near Ojo del Muerto, and Fort Cummins and Fort Seldon covered the southern approaches to the Jornados. Inside a year, the International Production Company of Philadelphia felt safe enough to pursue its investment. After all, even if the original cheque never had been cashed, the company still had its paper, giving it full and sole rights in the Stotter–Whitehead strike. It organized a work force that was guarded by three platoons of infantry out of Fort Seldon and a squadron of cavalry out of Fort Cummins; in addition, it hired thirty guns of its own: drifters and buffalo hunters and veterans from the Mexican war. The Army provided three field pieces, and when the Apaches tried to drive the invading force out of their territory, they got killed.

The miners and their protectors set up camp in the valley and began to work their way into the hills. It took another year before the lode began to produce any kind of worthwhile ore. By then a sizeable town had sprung up, lifting from the tents of the gamblers and whores and traders allowed in by the company to a spread of solid wooden buildings. The Apaches got mostly driven off, and after a while the Army reduced its contingents.

By the time the Civil War arrived, the town was named Green Springs, and was producing prime-grade ore at a very profitable rate. It was attacked three times during the War Between the States by Confederate forces, and more often by the Indians. The last attack was a joint effort: the Confederacy had succeeded in enlisting the Mimbrēnos to its cause.

The attack was beaten off when a massive force of Union troops arrived from Forts McRae, Cummins and Seldon. But by then the township of Green Springs was burned to the ground and most of the defenders were dead. The survivors got taken south to safety, and the mining company forgot the Stotter–Whitehead strike in favour of manufacturing armaments.

When the war ended, it took the company three years before it remembered it had an option on the gold. Then it sent a fresh team in and opened up the decaying shafts.

It got a shock: the gold was mostly worked out. The IPC took what it could before the output receded below a profitable margin, then it sold its interest to a man called Benjamin Parmalee. He was a rancher who had made a great deal of money trading cows to both sides during the Civil War. One of the few to anticipate the glut of cattle coming after, and the inevitable drop in prices, he took his money out of cows and put it into the town.

Under Parmalee's direction, Green Springs got rebuilt. The mine got opened up again, though on a much smaller scale —just enough to keep Ben Parmalee very wealthy—and it turned into the core of the settlement.

That was why wagon tracks ran down

the steep flanks of the valley's eastern edge and the rimrock was shrouded in a constant pall of smoke from the smelting sheds. It was why the Parmalee & Hansford Stage Company of New Mexico ran a link line with the Wells Fargo routes, and why there was a bank and a church and a regular jailhouse.

Ben Parmalee was sixty-nine years old, and looked fifty. He was tall and whipcord thin, with a thatch of thick silver hair and a mustache to match. He spent months of each year in St. Louis or Boston or even Washington, but when he came back to Green Springs—as he always did—he wore denim workpants and a faded shirt; like any of his miners. His first wife had died in the Civil War and his second had left him after he refused to move following the sixth Apache attack in seven months. He was childless, so all his energy got devoted to Green Springs.

He was a religious man who believed devoutly in the supremacy of the white race and his own right to make as much money as he possibly could. Niggers were put on the earth to serve and Indians were a menace that it was the duty of all right-thinking men to exterminate. Gold was a gift to those white men with the perspicacity and the courage to take it; more exactly, the gold in the Green Springs mine was his.

Tears coursed slowly down his tanned cheeks as he prayed. Beside him, staring at the stained-glass windows Parmalee had shipped in from New Orleans, Father Durant worried about the outcome of the robbery.

It was difficult to equate Parmalee's personal definition of right and justice with the teachings of the Father's church. Especially when the rancher had built this particular church and could get Durant dismissed to some god-forsaken mission in the wilderness simply by getting word to the church authorities back in St. Louis.

"Do not mourn their passing, friend." Durant set a hand cautiously on Parmalee's shoulder. "They died in course of their chosen duties. Good Christians, the loyal defenders of their master."

Parmalee shook the hand loose, opening his eyes. He saw the three corpses laid out on the trestle tables up in front of the altar, Grunted.

"Deserved to get killed," he said. His voice was low and harsh; like a cold wind blowing down from the north when the snows blocked the passes. "I hired those bastards on account of they was meant to be good. Then what? Christ! I ask you, Padre."

Father Durant smiled benignly and decided to say nothing: just let his patron continue.

"Four goddam no-account bums ride in an' lift one entire month's gold," snarled the rancher, answering his own question. "A goddam Mex, a fuckin' gambler, an' two cowboys. Ride in an' take the best month's output we had in two years. You know how much they got away with?"

Father Durant shook his head. Parmalee's knuckles got white as he gripped the pew.

"Nine thousand dollars' worth of refined gold," he rasped. "That's how much. Solid goddam ingots. Three wagon loads. An' all I got to show fer it is three fuckin' corpses and two men wrapped up in bandages that I gotta pay until they're healed an' ready to do a day's work again."

"The posse you sent out will surely find the miscreants," said Durant. "They cannot have gone far."

"Don't goddam need to go far around here," said Parmalee. "All they gotta do is hide the gold someplace. Stash it away an' then ride clear. Come back later to collect. Jesus!"

"God will visit justice upon them," murmured Durant. Then gasped and stepped back as the rancher stood up.

"God ain't fillin' my bank balance," said Parmalee. "It's the gold from my goddam mine that does that. What's the time?"

Without waiting for an answer, he thumbed a big gold Hunter from his vest and flicked the cover open. The hands stood at three minutes after four.

"Arrange to bury them, will you,

Father?" He flicked the watch closed and settled it back in his pocket. "I'm over to Sid's place fer a drink."

Durant nodded and watched the rancher stalk from the church. He sighed, conscience torn between condemnation of blood lust and the vague hope that it would be the law, rather than Parmalee's hired guns, that would catch them. At least that way they might be brought to fair trial before they got hung.

Green Springs was quiet as Parmalee left the church and headed towards the St. Lawrence Arms. All the able-bodied men in town—by which Parmalee meant those able to wield a pick or shoulder an ore wagon or handle a gun—were out looking for the four bandits. Sheriff Stoker had led a bunch of twelve men southwards, mostly Parmalee hands, and separate groups— each led by a hand-picked man—had gone north and east and west. Now the only people left around were the wet-belly storekeepers, the old folks and the women.

Parmalee spat, and dragged a sleeve

across his face; cursing. It was four days now since the raid, and so far only two riders had come back. To report that there was no sign of the thieves.

He went into the St. Lawrence Arms and settled his elbows on the bar.

Sid James dried his hands on a cloth and lifted a strand of lank hair clear of his gold-rimmed spectacles before opening a bottle of the good whisky and checking the glass was clean.

"Mister Parmalee." He grinned nervously as he set the liquor in front of the rancher. "Any word?"

Parmalee shook his head without speaking. Tossed off the whisky, and waited for James to pour him a second.

"They'll find them, mister Parmalee." He put more confidence into his voice than he felt. "They're bound to. That many men."

"Christ!" Parmalee emptied his second and stared at the barkeep. "You don't know horse apples from the kind that grow on trees, Sid. Stoker's gettin' soft from easy livin' an' the men I put out, they're more used to ridin' shotgun on a wagon than trackin' bandits. That's how come those godless fuckin' outlaws was able to down five of 'em an' ride clear with my money. You stick to those yellow paper stories you're always peddlin', an' leave the real worrying to me."

Sid James nodded, glancing nervously at the sheaf of paper tucked under the bar. His writing was mostly a joke to the people in Green Springs, but he had sold a few stories already, and he was confident that his latest would be a winner. He was basing it on a man he had once met, a cold, hard man who gave his name as John Ryker, but had granted James the right to call him Jack. A bounty hunter, a gunslinger. He thought Ryker would make a good subject for a novel.

"Bring the bottle over, will you?" Parmalee turned towards a table set against the wall. "Then leave me be."

Sid James nodded and hurried round the bar.

He set the bottle down in front of Parmalee and ambled over to the door. It was too early for the storekeepers to come in, but he hoped he might see one of the posses returning: business had been lousy for the last four days.

He didn't see a posse, but he did see a single rider. The man was hunched over the saddle of a big black horse and he rode it slowly, like he was hurting, or very, very tired. As he got closer, James realized that it was probably a combination of both. The man's left leg was held out stiff from the pony's side, and when he looked up, James saw that his eyes were hollow in his skull, the whites reddened, with deep, dark shadows in the sockets. A sprouting beard covered his jaw, almost thick enough to hide the ugly swelling along one side.

For a moment, the barkeep wondered why he was shaking his head, then realized that he was just shifting his gaze around, scanning the street as he rode up to the saloon.

Gunfighter, thought the barkeep. Not one of Parmalee's.

Then he saw the black glove on the left

hand and the cut-down shotgun on the left hip, and amended his thought: *Dangerous* gunfighter!

He ducked back inside, turning to call a warning to the old man.

"Rider comin', mister Parmalee! Looks like a gunslinger. Mean. He's hurt."

Parmalee stood up and loosened the Colt's Navy model in his holster. People had told him to trade the pistol for a newer model, but he had refused, choosing instead to compromise the familiarity of the gun by getting it rechambered for brass ready-mades. He went over to the door.

"Jesus!" he grunted. "He looks a mess."

Hawk eased down from the saddle and hitched the black horse to the rail. His left leg was stiff as he climbed the steps and he didn't like the way the long-haired man with the glasses, or the old cowboy with the silver hair were staring at him. He was weary; aching and hungry. Ready for a hot tub and a few slugs of whisky.

He pushed past them and went up to the bar.

Sid James looked at Parmalee, then scurried back behind the counter. Parmalee went back to his table.

Hawk said, "Whisky."

James poured him a shot from one of the ordinary bottles, the kind that didn't bother with labels. Hawk tipped it down his throat and dropped a coin on the bar.

"Another."

He took the second slower, easing round on his good leg to survey the empty saloon. His eyes caught Parmalee's and passed on: the old man looked fierce, but he also looked past it. Hawk dismissed him.

"You got a stable?"

James nodded. "Sure. Over behind the stage depot."

Hawk dropped some more coins. "Get someone to put my horse away. In a stall. He's hungry, so tell them to watch he don't bloat himself."

It didn't occur to Sid James to argue.

"Hotel yours, or someone else run that?" asked Hawk.

"Me." said James. "Me an' my wife."

"Good." Hawk drank more whisky. "I want a room an' a bath. Later, I'll want food."

"Fine. I'll see to that."

"Doctor?"

James looked at Hawk's face, then down at the weals circling his wrists: "Yeah. Doc Caughey."

Hawk waited, his eyebrows lifting to form an unspoken question.

"Next block down. Three doors along. You'll see the shingle outside." The words came out in a rush. "What happened to you? Looks like a mule train ran over you."

Hawk smiled. Cold. "Not mules; men. You seen a Mexican an' three Americans round here? Mex is short an' fat. Wears pearl-handle pistols, cross-draw. One of the whites favours a black suit an' a shoulder rig. The other two look like cowboys."

James mouth slacked open and his eyes darted automatically to Parmalee. The old man came up on his feet faster than most men half his age could move.

Hawk was faster still. His left hand opened, dropping the glass on to the bar. It bounced once, splashing the front of James's shirt as the gloved hand fastened on his long hair and yanked him forwards, dragging him across the counter. At the same time Hawk's right hand fisted the Colt out of the holster. He drew like John T. McLain had taught him: take the hammer back with the thumb while the gun's still clearing leather; use the cutaway to get your forefinger over the trigger. Then hold tight until the muzzle's pointed where you want the bullet to go.

Parmalee shrugged and let the Colt's Navy drop back under the leather.

"You're good, boy. Fast."

"Fast enough," said Hawk, "to kill you, old man. An' your tame barkeep."

"No need," said Parmalee. "Not unless the Mex an' his boys are friends of your'n."

Hawk grinned. It wouldn't have looked pretty, anyway. With the yellow-purple bruise on his jaw and the drying blisters on his face, it looked pure ugly. Evil.

"You seen them," he said. It wasn't a question. "When?"

"Four days since," said Parmalee. "They robbed me."

Hawk looked at him and wondered what Brava and his men might have taken from some beat-up old cowpoke. "Of what?" he demanded.

Parmalee grinned and pointed at Sid James. He was careful to keep both his hands up in the air.

"You can let Sid go, boy. He won't do nothin' lest I tell him. I own him along with most of this town. Name's Parmalee. Ben Parmalee."

Hawk looked at the barkeep from the corner of one reddened eye. James nodded as best he could with his face twisted sideways into a puddle of whisky.

"That's right," he mumbled, "mister Parmalee there owns the town an' the mine. Everything."

"Mine?" Hawk asked. "That why they come here?"

James tried to nod, and Parmalee said: "Three wagons loaded with prime gold. What they take from you?"

"Time," Hawk replied, letting loose the barkeep's hair so that James fell back from the counter and clattered the stacked bottles behind.

"Time?" he mumbled. "Is that all?"

"Time is of the essence," said Parmalee. "It's all a man's got to build on. He needs some comfort an' some courage, but I've found that in bottles of whisky. Time's what counts. It comes creepin' up on you like some old grey cat in winter an' afore you know it, you've lost your coat from the cold. Ain't nothin' worse you can steal from a man than time. Exceptin' gold."

Hawk set the hammer of the Colt to quarter cock. Turned the cylinder until the empty chamber was under the hammer, and then eased the pin down.

"Let's talk," said Parmalee. "I'll take you down to Doc Caughey's while Sid here gets yore pony stabled. We can maybe help each other."

"You just singing?" Hawk demanded. "Or you talking money?"

"I ain't whistlin' *Dixie*," said Parmalee.

"Then let's talk," said Hawk. "You're turning music into gold."

5

DOC CAUGHEY was a Canadian with a store-front surgery that opened out into a well-equipped operating room behind the black-curtained frontage. He was upwards of forty and had spent the last twenty years of his life wandering around the northern territories looking for somewhere to settle. When he saw an advertisement in a medical journal for a doctor to handle mining injuries in New Mexico he had come south after the job. He had experience in Montana and Washington. He was good: Ben Parmalee had hired him on the spot because he wanted an experienced man and because Caughey was closer to his own age than any of the other doctors who had bothered to apply. All three of them.

Parmalee had never mentioned that a doctor called Cade would have got the job if he hadn't been just moving through, so

Caughey had been around Green Springs for close on five years. And he had done good work.

He examined Hawk's injuries and announced them mostly healing.

"You took one godawful beating," he said, "but that's mending on its own. I'll fix you some salves to take the bruising down, and the blisters. The hip's something else: that'll take longer."

"I don't have longer," grunted Hawk. "Not long at all."

"Quit raving on," said Caughey, equably. "You just take your time and you'll be moving around like normal inside a week."

"I'm searching," grunted Hawk. "I don't have too long."

Parmalee chuckled from across the room. "Seems to me we're lookin' fer the same people. Me, I got around fifty men huntin' them on account o' the gold they stole. I'll make you a deal: you wait up the time Doc says an' I'll pay yore medical bills. If they don't show up by then, you go lookin' fer them. I'll pay you one thousand dollars on every one you bring back."

"Why?" Hawk winced as Caughey set a hot poultice on his naked hip. "That's close on half your bullion gone."

Parmalee shrugged. "Still leaves me five thousand, don't it? I can afford that. Besides, it sets a precedent. You bring them owlhooters back—dead or alive, or just plain evidence of their killing—an' it's gonna make every other bandit with a yen to take the Green Springs mine think twice."

"Yeah." Hawk nodded, pulling on his pants. "But why me?"

Parmalee shrugged again, thinking about what he had said to the Father. "My men are gettin' soft. They're used to guardin' wagons an' banks, but they ain't trackers. You follered that owlhoot gang clear through. Besides, you got a personal score to settle. It's like someone stepped on your shoes instead o' someone else's. I reckon that makes you all the keener to see 'em dead. Another thing: I saw you draw. You were good."

"I could be bad," said Hawk. "I could find them and take the gold for myself."

"Wouldn't be worth it." Parmalee shook his head. "Your name's Jared Hawk an' I know what you look like. You'd have problems shifting the gold. More sellin' it. An' all that time, you'd know I had Pinkertons after you."

Hawk grinned. "I think you got yourself a deal, Parmalee."

"I usually do." The old man nodded, his clear blue eyes unwinking. "That's why I'm the biggest thing around here."

"Yeah." Hawk believed him. "But you still got a whole lot of gold missing."

"Most idols got feet o' clay," said Parmalee. "Mine are just pure gold."

Hawk buttoned his shirt and followed the old man out of the doctor's place.

It was three days before the posses came back. Sunday. Father Durant was ringing the church bell and waiting for his congregation to gather. Hawk and Parmalee were sitting outside the St. Lawrence Arms, sipping beer and watching the street.

It was a hot, dusty day. The sun was slanting down out of a clear blue sky and a turn-about in the breeze was taking the stink out of the smelting sheds clear of Green Springs, blowing it away to the north. The town was quiet, the Father's flock made up of women and children and storekeepers. Beneath the clangor of the single bell there was an air of tension.

Hawk's bruises were healing well: the contusions on his wrists and ankles were fading into scar tissue, and his hip was solid. He could walk easily now, thanks to Doc Caughey's poultices and his own determination, and he was getting fretful.

The first posse came in as the bell stopped ringing and Father Durant cast one last, despairing glance down the street. It was led by a man in a sweat-stained blue shirt, who doffed his hat as he dismounted and looked too afraid to mount the stoop where Parmalee sat.

"Nothin', mister Parmalee." He wiped sweat from his face, his shirt sleeve rasping over the stubble. "Nothing at all."

"You done what you could, Wade."

Parmalee set his beer down on the planking of the porch. "Go on in an' get yourself a drink. All of you! On me."

Sid James smiled and began to set glasses and mugs out on the bar, enjoying his first worthwhile custom in a week.

His enjoyment got bigger and better as the groups came in. They all reported the same: no sign of the outlaws, nor any of the gold. Seven days of scanning trail had brought nothing but thirst and weariness: they were glad to get back to town and spend money in the saloon.

"Looks like you don't make that reward," said Parmalee. "Looks like they're off an' gone."

"Not from me," Hawk answered. "I got a debt to fill."

"My boys ain't the greatest trackers I know," said the mine owner, "but if them outlaws was around, they must've left tracks."

Hawk shrugged and tilted his mug against his mouth: his voice was slurred with foam when he said, "Who's this?"

"Jesus!" Parmalee stood up, staring

down the street at a fat man on a pale grey horse. "That's Stoker."

The sheriff was slumped low in his saddle. His head drooped down over his chest and he looked like a man riding in his sleep. His horse looked the same. Its neck hung low and it moved its hooves like a kitten on hot tiles. Froth plastered its nostrils, and long streamers of spittle dangled from its lips. Behind the peace officer there was a group of ten men in much the same condition.

Behind them, wrapped up in blankets and waterproof groundsheets, were two more men.

They were slung over the saddles of a roan and a palamino. They were lashed in place; wrists and ankles were linked by the strings connecting them under the horses' bellies. Despite the movement of the horses, flies clustered thick about the wrapped bodies.

Stoker climbed down off his horse and tossed the reins to the closest man. He climbed the stoop like an ancient: fat, rheumatic and weary.

"Well?" Parmalee emptied his beer and tossed the mug to one of the cowboys come out to watch. "What happened?"

The peace officer looked thirstily at the batwings and shrugged, wobbling folds of flesh around his jowls and belly.

"They headed south like you said, mister Parmalee. All the way to Blanco Canyon. Then they split up. Took three separate trails out. I sent men to check each one, but they all came together south o' the canyon. Went straight fer the border. Down towards Las Cruces they split off. Time I got the men regrouped, they'd gone over into Mexico."

"Jesus Christ!" snarled Parmalee. "They left tracks, didn't they? You must know where they're headed?"

"I'd guess Calaveros," said Stoker. "That's a pretty wild town. Whole lotta outlaws go there after crossin' the line."

"But you didn't follow them?" snarled Parmalee. "That thought never crossed your mind?"

"How could I?" Stoker touched the

five-pointed star on his sweaty shirt "I ain't got no jurisdiction there."

Parmalee shook his head and pointed at the two corpses.

"Who are they?"

"Dave Banner an' Colby Smith," said Stoker. "Dave got killed when the outlaws 'bushed us in cane country, just north o' the line. Then Colby got shot when he crossed the river."

"And the gold?" Parmalee asked. "What happened to my gold?"

Stoker's fat face burst out in a fresh spill of sweat. He fidgeted with his star.

"Why we took so long, mister Parmalee. Way I read the tracks, they left one wagon in Blanco Canyon an' took the other two south. By the time we reached Las Cruces, they'd dropped the second. The third looked like it crossed the border."

"An' you never found a single one o' them?" said Parmalee. "Not one o' those heavy-loaded wagons?"

Stoker ducked his head like a fat vulture embarrassed at finding only an empty corpse.

"No, sir! Not one. They just went like the ground swallowed them up. I did my best: I followed on far as I could. But those wagons are gone."

"Jesus fuckin' Christ!" rasped Parmalee. "I could hire St. Louis street-sweepers'd do a better job than you. Send the others into the saloon, I want to talk in yore office."

Stoker's fat face got pale, and fresh beadings of sweat came out from his forehed and cheeks. He waved his posse inside the saloon and followed Parmalee and Hawk down the board-walk to the jail.

"You recognize them?" Parmalee asked. "Any of them?"

"Luis Brava," said Hawk, "a fat little Mexican. Running with his brother and three Americans. Only the brother's dead now."

Stoker fumbled through a drawerful of dodgers, and began to peel posters on to his desk.

"Luis Brava," he said. "He's wanted for bank robbery in Texas and Arizona.

Six hundred dollars reward. There's a note appended, says he usually runs with his brother, Federico: he's worth five hundred."

"You owe me," said Hawk. "I killed him. What about the others?"

Stoker shook his head: "Nothing. All I know about Brava is he raids over the border an' then runs back into Mexico."

Hawk shrugged and looked at Parmalee. "So I go south. Calaveros sounds likely."

"Find him," said the mine owner. "You find him an' the others. Bring them back an' find where my gold is."

"Yeah," said Hawk. "I'll do it as best I can. I don't know no other way"

6

CALAVEROS lay south and west of El Paso, a sprawl of adobe buildings running along the shallow bank of Lake Guzman.

The lake formed a blue background to the white of the adobe bricks and the clearer colour of the sky. None of the buildings were taller than one storey, and where the sandy sides of the water sloped down into the blue they appeared even smaller: miniature houses huddling down like frightened children seeking cover from the blankness of the empty country around.

There was a central plaza, a small square with a tired fountain at the centre that bled a trickle of greenish water down over the two bowls surrounding the pedestal. Both bowls were plastered with bird droppings. Around the plaza there were a few palmettos, the fronds withering in the late summer heat, covered, like the edges of the fountain, with guano. Facing on to the plaza was a cantina and a Rurale station. The cantina looked dusty and quiet; the Rurale station looked deserted.

Hawk rode in and halted the black horse, staring round at the dusty-windowed stores and the tired faces watching him.

A man in a dirty khaki tunic with a sweat-darkened kepi pitched back over his greasy curls came to greet him. He carried a Mannlicher rifle on its strap over his shoulder, and his dark eyes were more worried than authoritative.

"Señor?" His voice was soft; nervous. *"Que pasa?"*

"Nada," said Hawk. *"Ni por pienso."*

"Then why are you here?" The man brushed a lazy hand over his sleeve, exposing the chevrons of a *sarjento*. "What do you want?"

"A man called Luis Brava," said Hawk. "I want to speak with him."

The Rurale's face got suddenly creased up with frown lines. He began to chew on his mustache, and the Mannlicher seemed to slide by accident down his shoulder. Just far enough that the stock fell into his hand and he caught it in time to leave the barrel pointing at Hawk's chest.

"What do you want with Luis?"

Hawk looked at the rifle. Then at the man's face. He smiled.

"I'm going to kill him," he said. "For no reason that concerns you."

"I am not sure I can let you do that," said the Rurale sergeant. "I don't know that I can let some *gringo* come riding in to kill a *compadre.*"

"He's here then," said Hawk. "Where?"

"Why should I tell you?" said the soldier. "Why do you want to kill him?"

"He tried to kill me," Hawk replied. "He staked me out and left me to die."

"You must be the one who shot Federico," said the Rurale. "I heard about that."

"Will you tell me where he is?" Hawk asked again. "Or are you hiding him?"

"I am hiding nothing, *señor.*"

As he said it, biting down on the words at the same time as he spat his mustache clear of his lips, the soldier squeezed the trigger of the rifle. Hawk sensed the movement and slid over the right side of the black horse. He flipped his feet loose from the stirrups and drew his Colt in a single blur of movement.

There was a flash of flame that stabbed like lightning through the cloud of black powder smoke, and the horse squealed and began to buck.

Hawk landed on his back, the Colt angled out over his chest, pointing between the horse's legs. He squeezed the trigger.

Saw the Rurale stagger back and squeezed it again.

The Mexican screamed and dropped his hands from the bolt of the rifle. He touched the spreading flower of red that was adding a different stain to his tunic, neatly between the buttons, where the Sam Browne belt crossed his chest. He tottered back. Behind him, a thick droplet of blood landed in the dust. Hawk's second shot struck higher than the first. It hit the Rurale's chest and deflected off the bone to drive upwards into his face. It left a bloody swathe along his chest and then disappeared beneath the overhang of his jaw. The Mexican's head jerked back and from the rear of his skull there emerged a great gobbet of blood and bone and sticky grey brain matter. He closed his eyes and fell spread-eagled in the dust.

Hawk ignored him, knowing he was dead, and rolled clear of the prancing horse as fresh bullets blasted dust and blood around him.

He twisted on to his belly, firing blind at the source of the attack. Emptied his gun and stumbled for the cover of the central fountain as the ambushers grouped back inside the cantina.

When he reached the fountain he hauled the Meteor shotgun clear of the holster and set the ugly weapon on the rim. Then he snapped the loading gate of the Colt open and began to work the ejector rod to drive the spent shells clear of the chambers. Bullets chipped splinters from the marble of the fountain before he had six fresh cartridges thumbed into the cylinders, and a man in blue denim was charging wild across the plaza with a Colt's Peacemaker blowing flame and death in front.

Hawk finished loading the Colt and fired twice. His first shot hit the man in the belly, doubling him, like a folded ruler, over his own length. The second hit as he was going down. It ploughed into the back of his neck, tearing through the spinal column to pierce a lung and lodge against the pelvis.

The man went down on his face with thick spurts of crimson gouting from his mouth and nostrils. The Colt he was holding fell clear of his spreading hand, and the fingers dug deep into the sand, nails breaking to add a thinner streaming of blood to the overlay of his skidding body.

Hawk fired back at the cantina. A window shattered and from somewhere inside a man screamed.

He reloaded the Colt.

More bullets splintered the fountain.

"I want Luis Brava," he yelled. "Send him out to face me! Or is he afraid?"

"He ain't here," shouted a voice Hawk didn't recognize. "You're just wastin' yore time."

"Who're you?" Hawk bellowed, getting angry. "One of his sidekicks? One of the cowardly bastards who pegged me out?"

"Yeah," shouted the unseen man. "I got yore feet! You looked good out there."

Pure rage burst inside Hawk's skull. It was as though all the blisters and boils and pain of his staking-out had festered inside his mind until they formed a core of pus-filled hate. And the only way to burst the pain was by taking away its source.

He thumbed a fresh shell into the Colt. Holstered the pistol, and picked up the shotgun.

He wriggled along the full length of the fountain and then lifted to his feet and ran, half-stumbling, to the cover of the porch that spanned the southern side of the plaza. A woman stared at him from behind the fly-specked glass of a store-front window. Then turned away and tugged curtains down over the frontage when she saw his face.

He moved on, holding against the shadow of the porches until he came to a section where a side alley bled out into the plaza.

Bullets drummed splinters from over his head as he crossed the gap and he triggered the Colt three times at the doorway of the cantina, then ran on to the corner of the square.

When he came to the angle of buildings that fronted the cantina he paused and reloaded his Colt. He dropped the pistol back inside the holster and lifted the cutdown Meteor into his right hand. His numbed left hand clutched the barrel, the stiffened fingers wrapping tight against the counterpointing grasp of the thumb. His right took the hammer back and closed down on the trigger.

He crossed the gap that divided the buildings, slinking sidelong towards the cantina. There was an alleyway that produced a trio of snarling dogs, then a nervous footage past a dry goods store.

And then a man in a wide sombrero and a fancy jacket came out from the cantina with a Colt's Cavalry model in his hand.

Hawk squeezed off the Meteor and saw the man gust away backwards, lifted up on the wave of Ten-gauge that spread in a diamond pattern through his chest and belly and ribs.

The man cannoned back against the frontage of the building, leaving long streamers of blood over the walls, and fell down on to the stoop. He rolled once, just far enough that his arm fell across the rim of the porch and hung from the ledge. Blood ran down his sleeve and collected over his hand until it was thick enough to drip from his fingers and make five pools of fly-bait in the dust.

Hawk reloaded the Meteor and went on across the gap dividing him from the cantina. Each step he took was like putting a foot in a grave. He expected bullets to hit him from the blank windows and the rooftops. Expected to die.

And knew that he couldn't do anything but keep pressing on.

He reached the frontage of the cantina and ducked under the window. Got down on his belly and worked his way to the doors.

He stuck the Meteor under the batwings and shouted, "I want Luis Brava!"

A voice that was hoarse with either fear or outrage shouted, "He ain't here."

Hawk said, "You got a back door?"

"Yeah."

"Then get to it, fast!" He rolled across the frontage as he spoke the words. "I'm firing now."

There was the sound of bootheels clattering on the planks. The sound of men running. He triggered the scattergun, spreading a wide swathe of shot down the length of the cantina.

A man screamed. Hawk stood up and ran around the angle of the building, reloading the shotgun as he moved. He reached the back entrance and watched the survivors come out: they were Mexican, and none looked like Luis Brava.

He cocked the Meteor and stepped up on to the porch that held the cantina up from the dusty ground. There was a single narrow door with sprays of beads announcing the exit of the drinkers as they glistened and clattered in the fading sunlight.

Hawk stepped through them.

And came into a narrow hallway with doors opening off on both sides.

There was a smell of chili and tequila and a second door that opened on to the main room of the cantina. It was a narrow door, more narrow than the spread of two batwings, but a little larger than the breadth of a hotel door.

It was open. And beyond the square of light there was a man.

He held a Winchester carbine in his hands, and he was staring out through the opening of the batwings. He was dressed in denim pants and a matching shirt. Long red hair spilled over his collar, and his gunbelt was hiked round to his left hip.

Hawk said, "Where's Luis gone?"

The man turned around and froze.

"You killed Wade," he said. "That was you out there."

"Yeah." Hawk nodded. "I guess so. Don't make the same mistake."

The redhead shrugged: "You musta caught him unexpected. Same as the Mex."

"You ain't exactly primed," said Hawk, shifting the scattergun. "Or can you beat this?"

"I reckon to put one slug into you," said the red-haired man. "One at least."

"I doubt it," said Hawk.

And went down on his face with the Meteor spreading an ugly pattern of heavy gauge shot across the floor. Where the denim-clad outlaw's feet would be.

The Meteor gouted a cloud of dark smoke that was roiled by the passage of the .44 calibre slug that blasted from the muzzle of the Winchester. Hawk sensed, rather than heard, the bullet pass above him, thudding dully into the adobe of the cantina's rear wall. The sound of impact was lost beneath the guttural scream of the outlaw.

Hawk had deliberately angled the shotgun's muzzle down towards the floor. Had he aimed his shot a few inches higher, the pellets would have ripped the man's legs apart, nervous shock and loss of blood killing him instantly. As it was, at least half the force of the discharge ploughed into the boards, tearing a yard-long swathe of splinters up in a cloud of dust and wood chips. The upper edge of the diamond pattern hit the outlaw's feet and ankles. His denim pants fluttered, tatters of blood-stained blue cloth waving in the artificial breeze. His boots seemed to fold in against the fragile flesh beneath, holes appearing that spattered thin droplets of blood over the floor. He went on screaming as he dropped the rifle and toppled sideways

When he hit the floor his screaming died to a low, deep groaning and he curled in a foetal ball with both hands pressed about his ankles. Blood pulsed from between his fingers.

Hawk rolled sideways, transferring the

Meteor to his left hand as he drew the Colt.

He swung the pistol in a wide arc, covering the front entrance and the bar and the rear door. From behind the bar there came a voice.

"*Pistolero? Señor?*" It quavered on the brink of hysteria. "Can I come out? I am not armed."

"Move," Hawk grunted, climbing to his feet. "*Pero manos altos.*"

The barkeep came out with both hands stretching to touch the ceiling. He was short and skinny, with a bald patch that glistened as pure terror pushed sweat through the pores.

"You alone?" Hawk asked.

The man nodded. "*Si, señor pistolero.* All alone. The others they went out the back."

"Tell them to stay out," rasped the gunfighter. "I got business to discuss. I get mad if I'm disturbed."

"*Si, señor.*" The barkeep nodded enthusiastically and began to move for the rear. "I will tell them."

"Wait!" Hawk glanced out through the batwings. "There are more Rurales in town?"

"No, *señor*." The barkeep shook his head, the movement spraying droplets of sweat from his face. "The sergeant was the only one."

"Good," said Hawk. "Get out."

He waited until the little man was gone through the rear door and then went over to the outlaw.

The man was still curled up, his face pale and his red hair damp with sweat. His hands clutched his ankles as though he thought the pressure of his fingers might hold in the pain.

"What's your name?" Hawk asked.

"Charlie Braco. Christ! You goddam crippled me. I ain't ever gonna walk right again."

"Where's Brava?"

"I don't know! I swear to God I don't know."

Hawk sniffed and set the Colt down on the floor. He broke the Meteor open and tugged the spent cartridge clear of the breech. Thumbed a fresh load in and holstered the scattergun. Then he picked up the Colt and tapped the barrel against the outlaw's left ankle. Braco screamed.

"You lifted three wagons loaded with gold," said Hawk. "You an' Brava an' the others. A whole lotta gold. You ain't had time to sell it, so you must know where the others are. Tell me."

He emphasized his question by dropping the barrel of the Colt on to the man's right foot. Braco screamed again.

"Jesus! I don't know fer sure. I swear it! I ain't lyin'."

"What do you know?" Hawk asked. "Tell me."

Braco began to weep. His mouth twisted into a down-curving line and his eyes screwed tight shut, tears running from under the lids. His body trembled.

"There was five of us," he moaned. "Luis an' Federico. Cole Vansittart. Me an' Wade Strother. You killed Federico an' Wade. Guess you're gonna kill me now."

"Maybe not," said Hawk slowly.

"Maybe I'll leave you live. Depends what you tell me."

It came out in a rush. Braco was too far gone into pain and fear to hold anything back: he spoke freely.

"We split up," he moaned, "soon after the raid. Luis an' Cole stashed a wagon in Blanco Canyon. I don't know where, because me an' Wade was takin' the other two on. Cole set that up. He knew someone in Green Springs. That was how we knew it was a good time to hit the mine. The idea was they left some o' the gold there to divvy up later. The feller Cole knew was in fer a share."

"Where's Cole?" Hawk snarled. "Where's Brava?"

"I'm gettin' to that." Braco went on clutching his ruined ankles. "Oh, Jesus! I hurt. We met up again north of Las Cruces. There's a box canyon five miles out of the town. Entrance is real narrow. Mostly covered with scrub. It was some old Indian burial ground; something like that. The end was all filled with caves. That's where we put the second wagon.

There's a real big cave faces due west. Sun hits it right inside when it's goin' down. The wagon's in the smaller cave right underneath."

"That's two," said Hawk. "You want to try for the third?"

"Oh God!" Braco said. "I told you about two o' them, an' just one could set you up fer life. Ain't that enough?"

"No," said Hawk. And dropped the full weight of the Colt down over the man's ankles.

Braco bit off a scream. "Suppose we split it? That was the idea when we started. Me an' Wade sharin' the one wagon. Luis an' Cole was splittin' the other two with Cole's buddy."

"I made some promises," said Hawk. "I promised myself I'd find Brava, an' I told a man in Green Springs I'd find his gold. I don't like breaking my word."

Braco gave in to the inevitable, and said: "It's in the stable behind this place. We hid the gold under a pile o' fodder. You let me go now? I need a doctor."

Hawk shook his head. "No. I still want Brava. And Cole Vansittart. Where are they?"

"God!" moaned Braco. "I ain't sure. We fixed to meet in Las Cruces one month hence. End o' the month. I don't know where they'd be now."

"That's all right," said Hawk, standing up. "You given me enough to find them. And most of the gold. Thanks."

"You gonna take it?" asked Braco. "All of it?"

"Gonna take it back to Green Springs," said Hawk. "That's what I got paid for. That and killing you."

He slid the Colt down into the holster and began to walk towards the batwings. Behind him, Charley Braco snuffled and spat. And then there was the sound he had expected. The sound he was waiting for.

It was the soft movement of metal against leather: the noise of a gun getting drawn from the holster.

Hawk didn't bother drawing the Colt. He ducked forwards with his right hand crossing his waist to fasten on the pistol grip of the shotgun. Thumbed the hammer back and squeezed the trigger. The Meteor bounced in his hand and a flash of heat burst against his hip.

Charley Braco opened his mouth to scream as he saw the muzzle flash, but he never got time to release the sound. His open mouth took most of the force of the Ten-gauge shot. His lips and cheeks and jaw were spread apart, reduced to flying tatters of skin and sinew. His teeth got shattered, fragments flying back into a tongue that was already curling up and tearing apart. The skin was flayed clear of his face, leaving white outlines of bone that were immediately painted red. The back of his throat opened up to release the chunks of bone and teeth that burst clear of the thick column of blood gouting from the severed veins and arteries in his opened neck. His head jerked back, one eye dulling as ruptured blood vessels stained the white; the other plopped loose from the socket, dangling down over his cheek as his face got crimson and slumped sideways on to his shoulder. Like the head of a puppet when the controller lets go the strings.

Hawk turned, opening the shotgun to pluck the spent shell clear and thumb a fresh load in.

He looked at the ravaged corpse and shook his head.

"That's the trouble with gold, Charley. It goes right to a man's head."

He went out to the plaza and collected his horse, then led it round to the back of the cantina and located the wagon. The people he had driven out gathered to watch him, though no one ventured near and none tried to stop him.

He hefted the fodder clear of the vehicle and found a roped-down tarpaulin. When he lifted a corner, he saw the dull gleam of gold ingots. He fetched four mules from the stalls and because no one questioned his taking them, assumed they were the original team. They settled into the traces easily enough and he hitched his own mount to the

tail. Then took the wagon out of Calaveros, heading north. Back to Green
Springs.

7

"TWO thousand dollars. I'll take yore word they're dead."

Parmalee slapped the notes on the table and pushed the wad over to Hawk. The gunfighter nodded his thanks and folded the wad into his pocket.

"What you gonna do about the others?"

Hawk shrugged. "Go looking, I guess. I can find the second wagon, so I'll most likely find Brava or Vansittart."

"How about the third man?" said Parmalee. "The goddam bastard's been selling me out?"

"One of the others should point me to him," said Hawk. "Braco said it was Vansittart set the thing up, so I should get a lead there."

"I hope so," said Parmalee. "You want another drink?"

Hawk shook his head. "No. I want some sleep."

He stood up, crossing the plush carpet that covered the mine owner's suite of rooms in the St. Lawrence Arms hotel and opened the door.

"When you leavin'?" Parmalee asked. "You need anything?"

"Morning," said Hawk. "Nothing."

The corridor was lit softly by the dim glow of kerosene lamps spaced out in brackets down the length of carpeted hallway. There was a dull murmur of sound from the rooms below, and a faint, rich odour of cigar smoke. Hawk's own room was one of the best he had seen, adjacent to the suite where Parmalee lived, and larger than most. There was a big, wide bed occupying the centre, with a tub set against one corner, surrounded by a fancy Chinese screen and equipped with genuine taps that fed genuine water into the tub. If he wanted it hot, he still had to ask for buckets to be brought up from the kitchen, but the taps could be turned to produce cold, and that was a giant step forwards for most Western hotels.

Parmalee had told him the room was mostly reserved for personal friends or influential guests: ore buyers, or senators; the kind of prominent Eastern folk the mine owner needed to butter up. The previous month, he had told Hawk, there was a senator from Georgia staying over. A farmer with designs on the White House. His name was James Carter, and he owned a lot of land in the South, but to pursue his ambitions he needed the support of Western money.

"What'd you tell him?" Hawk had asked. "You fund his campaign?"

Parmalee had shrugged and said, "Peanuts. Man'd jump at sight of a rabbit. Looked like one, come to think on it."

The gunfighter unlocked the door and stepped inside the room. The curtains had been drawn and the bed turned down. Beside the tub there were two pails with sealed covers, the exteriors sweating evaporated moisture down the zinc sides. That was the kind of care afforded Parmalee's guests.

Hawk locked the door behind him and

stripped out of his clothes. He thought about taking a bath, but then decided to leave it for the morning. Instead he poured a mug of coffee from the pot beside his bed and checked over his guns.

When he was finished, he poured a second cup of coffee and filled a glass with whisky. It was the first time in three weeks he had relaxed.

The ride up from Calaveros had been uneventful in the long term, but he had spent each moment of it tensed for a bullet, waiting for pursuit from the border town or an ambush from ahead. Nothing had happened, and in a way that he didn't bother to explain to himself or anyone else, it was disappointing. The build-up of tension had lifted him on to a peak of awareness that had folded into anticlimax when nothing happened. He was keyed up in mind and body, and the release of violence might have leavened that tension.

As it was, he felt fidgety, nervous.

He tucked his Colt under the pillows and set the shotgun on the floor. The wad of notes Parmalee had given him went into his saddlebags that he tossed inside the wardrobe.

He drank the whisky and climbed into the bed.

And there was a knock on his door.

He slid smoothly from under the sheets, right hand fisting the Colt. The hammer came back as he crossed the carpet and slid against the wall on the left side of the door. He reached out to turn the key, not exposing his body.

"Yeah? What you want?"

"Mister Hawk?" The voice was feminine. Soft and slightly embarrassed. "Mister Jared Hawk?"

He opened the door. And a woman gasped, fluttering a red-nailed hand over her mouth in parody of surprise.

She was in her twenties, naturally blonde hair piled up, French style, above an oval face that was mostly taken up with wide eyes and wider mouth. She wore a dark blue dress that reached down to her ankles from a low start: it nipped in over her waist and appeared to be supported by nothing more than gravity where it crossed her cleavage. A thin band of matching material circled her throat, fastened at the front by a small cameo. Then silver earrings hung down from under her golden locks. Her right wrist supported a small bag.

Hawk ducked his head out into the corridor: it was empty, so he waved the girl in.

"Well," she said, in a Southern accent, "I do declare."

"What?" Hawk closed the door and turned the key.

"Mister Parmalee said you were a gunfighter, but I never knew you'd have so many weapons. And so big."

Her eyes fluttered coyly over the Colt in Hawk's hand and the shotgun on the floor; and his body.

"Parmalee sent you?" he asked. "Why?"

"Why do you think?" she asked. "Ours not to reason why; ours but to . . . well . . . try, I guess. Don't you want to?"

"Want to what?" asked Hawk. "Quit talking riddles."

"That wasn't a riddle, mister Hawk. Or may I call you Jared?" She sat down on the bed. "That was a poem. A very good poem. I can't remember much more, but it's about people doing things they want to. Do you want me?"

The simplicity of statement took Hawk by surprise. Most of the whores he had slept with acted out a pantomime of coyness, or spread their assets on the line, no questions asked or answered. This girl acted something different.

"I guess," he said. "Yeah."

"Good. I've never been with a real gunfighter before." She dropped her bag on the floor, by the head of the bed, and began to undress. "I hope you're all right."

"I'll do my best," said Hawk.

"I hope so," said the girl, standing up. "Will you help me with my dress, please?"

Hawk began to unhook the eyes running down the back. As he worked on them, the girl reached up to tug the pins holding her hair in place loose. A mane of sweetly-scented blonde curls fell down past the gunfighter's face as the dress came away from her hips.

"Thank you," she said. "Would you hang it up for me, please?"

Hawk nodded dumbly and carried the dress over to the wardrobe. He opened the doors and fetched a hanger out. Set the dress on the curved wood and hooked the metal pin on the rail. When he turned back, after closing the doors, the girl was naked, stretched languorously over the down-turned sheets.

She was surprisingly full breasted, the nipples standing hard against the softer flesh and the dark circles of her aureoles. Her waist was trim, fading into rounded thighs that flowed like running honey into long legs. Between them there was a patch of dark honey hair.

She smiled and stretched back against the pillows, rolling her body so that Hawk was visited a glance at every plane of flesh, each crevice and declivity.

"Don't you want me?" she asked. "Don't you like me?"

"What I see," he rasped. "What's your name?"

"Johanna," she said. "You like what you see?"

Hawk crossed the room in three fast strides and came on to the bed.

"I'm seeing visions, Johanna," he mumbled, burying his face in her hair. "And they feel good."

"I'm glad," she said. "That's how it should be."

She was warm and soft and demanding, leading him down avenues of pleasure that left him gasping with exhausted delight. For a while he forgot his pains, forgot his hate, forgot his mission. He gave himself up to the ministrations of her body, letting everything else wash away on the long wave of pleasure she brought him.

He slept. It was easy in the big, soft bed, with the girl wrapped warm against him. It was the first time in three weeks. Longer since he had enjoyed a woman: he slept soundly.

It was the absence of warmth that woke

him. That and the pale light filtering in through the curtained windows He stirred under the soiled sheets, right hand shifting automatically beneath the pillows. To where the Colt should have been.

Two things registered in his mind at the same time: the girl was gone and the Colt wasn't there. He sat up.

The room was dim, grey under the pale light of early dawn, shadowy. It was hard to see, because his eyes were fogged with sleep and pleasure, misted with a fog of exhaustion and sex. Across the room a faint shape wafted back and forth before the wardrobe. Hawk saw his saddlebags lifted out.

He sat up and reached down to where his shotgun should be. It wasn't there.

"Stay where you are, Jared!" He froze as Johanna's voice cut like a knife through the dawn stillness. "I don't want to kill you, but I will if I must."

"Why?" he said. "You with Brava?"

"No." Her fair hair twirled loose as she shook her head. "Not that greaser bandit."

"Then why?" Hawk asked again. "What you playing at?"

"It needn't concern you," she muttered. "Just stay still and leave me be. We won't bother you again."

"We?" Hawk saw the small outline of a Remington derringer in her hand and calculated the chances of jumping her. The tiny pistol was a killer over ten or fifteen feet, the .41 calibre slug capable of stopping a man dead. "Who's *we*?"

"Leave it," she said. "It doesn't concern you.'

"No," he muttered, "I guess it don't."

And spun a pillow across the room as he powered clear of the bed.

Johanna fired wild as the pillow lifted towards her. The derringer blasted flame that scorched the cotton cover and then Hawk was on her.

He came down in a wild dive that carried him under the Remington's aim. Fastened his arms around her hips and dragged her down on to the floor. He tasted the sweetly-sour aftermath of sex as her thighs fastened about his face. And then a knee hit him between the eyes.

He closed them, reaching up to grab for her wrists. Johanna brought the butt of the derringer down hard against his skull, and fountains of bright sparks burst over his eyes. Then a knee rammed hard and practised into his groin and his belly got filled with fire that threatened to roil up through his chest and spill out of his mouth. He groaned and doubled over, still fighting to hold on to the girl's wrists.

She kicked him again and hammered the derringer against his hands. Cursing, he felt his fingers open as he brought his knees up to protect his manhood.

Johanna broke loose. She dropped the saddlebag as she ran for the door. Wailed when she found it locked. Turned to the window.

Her heels drummed over Hawk's back as she crossed the room and began to fight the catch open. Hawk opened his eyes and saw the Colt on the floor in front of him. After that it was just pure instinct.

He got his fingers around the butt.

Thumbed the hammer back as his forefinger closed on the trigger. The muzzle was lined on Johanna's back as she got the window open and began to clamber through.

Hawk squeezed the trigger.

The Colt bucked in his hand, wafting a single lightning flash of smoking death across the room. Johanna screamed once as the bullet hit her between the shoulders, slamming through the ribs to puncture a lung and emerge through the centre of her right breast. An inch-wide plucking of material tore loose from her dress, curving out across the street as a small fragment fell loose: her right nipple.

The piece of flesh hit the dirt before the material. Before her body, thrust forwards under the discharging power of the Colt, crashed against the window frame. Her head struck the upper rim, teeth and nose shattering against the wood so that splinters of glass fragmented back into her eyes and checks. Her body doubled over, the slender waist buckling forwards under the impact of the bullet as her hands spread

140

wide, nails splitting and breaking as they clutched the window's rim.

Then she pitched forwards, slithering down over the roof of the porch to land in the street. Where her hands had gripped the window there were deep marks in the soft wood, all stained with blood. Where her body hit the dirt there was a great blister of crimson, more spreading slowly from under her face. The porch was marked by a long, glistening trail of scarlet.

Hawk watched the people gather around her corpse and thumbed the spent shell clear of the cylinder. He reloaded the pistol. Picked up the shotgun from inside the wardrobe, and checked his money. Then he began to dress.

He had his pants and shirt on before the pounding on his door began. His gunbelt fastened around his waist.

When he opened the door he saw Ben Parmalee and Sheriff Stoker staring at him. Parmalee was holding the Colt's Navy model revolver, Stoker had a full-sized Winchester shotgun with both hammers back.

"You got some questions to answer," he said. "The replies better be good."

Hawk shrugged. "She was a night-time woman. Come dawn she just went out."

"Through the window?" grated the peace officer. "With a bullet in her back?"

"The nature of her profession," said Hawk. "In an' out fast."

8

"I GOTTA lock him up, mister Parmalee." Stoker said. "I ain't got no choice."

"She tried to kill him, Buford." Parmalee's piercing blue eyes fastened on the lawman's face. "You saw the derringer she was carryin'. You saw the hole in the wall. He was actin' in self-defence."

"Maybe." Stoker swung his chair around to direct a glance at the cells. To where Hawk stood behind bars. "Maybe he'll get off. But until a judge an' a duly appointed court says he's innocent, I gotta hold him."

"Christ Jesus!" Parmalee shook his head. "I hired him to find my gold, Buford. He's already brought one wagon back, an' that was more'n you could do. You keep him locked up here, those goddam outlaws are gonna ride clear. That ain't gonna look good fer you when election time comes. You thought on that?"

"I thought on that, mister Parmalee," said the fat lawman, "an' I still come up with the same answer. Ain't no one gonna put a vote in my direction if I let a woman-killer go. Heistin' gold's one thing; gunning a woman is something else."

"She was a whore," said Parmalee. "A piece of trash. She sold her body to the highest bidder."

"She was what Father Durant might call a lost soul," admitted Stoker. "But where's the difference between her an' yore hired man? I seen gunfighters before, an' they ain't much more'n killing machines. You hired him to do a job for you, same as you'd hire someone to fix a fence or mend a plough. Johanna was hired the same way. Difference was she got killed."

"Someone did hire her," called Hawk. "You think about that?"

"I thought about it," said Stoker. "I thought about it a whole lot. But I ain't detailed to make decisions on right an' wrong: that's fer the judge to decide."

"An' he won't be here in weeks," said Parmalee. "Meanwhile, my gold gets taken."

"You could send yore own men to find it," suggested Stoker. "You got the directions."

Parmalee shook his head. "I got most of 'em watchin' the sheds. Word's out that I got took heavy, so there's every goddam outlaw in the territory thinkin' to do the same. Besides, I gotta make up the loss, an' that means a whole new batch of ore goin' through, which'll need guarding. Besides, if I send a posse down to Las Cruces the law there's gonna get finickity."

"You got a point, mister Parmalee," Stoker allowed. "But there ain't a thing I can do about that. I got my duty as a legally appointed peace officer, an' right now that means holdin' this feller in jail."

"Jesus!" Parmalee stood up. "I'll pay his bail. How much you want? A thousand? Two?"

"Nossir. I don't want nothin'." Stoker climbed ponderously to his feet. "I can't allow this man out. He's gotta wait fer the judge to come round."

"Shit! You just lost the next election," said Parmalee. "I'll make it my business to see you kicked out on yore fat arse."

"As you like, mister Parmalee." Stoker wiped a hand over his fleshy lips. "That's yore choice. Mine is to do my duty."

"Shit!" Parmalee halted at the door, turning to call across the room to where Hawk was draped over the bars. "I'll see what I can do, boy. Don't you worry none."

The door swung shut behind him with a finality that sent little shivers of nervousness down the gunfighter's spine. Stoker turned around, his flabby face wreathed in an ugly smile.

"Looks like you'll be waitin' some time, gunman. Be six weeks afore the judge gets here. Best make yoreself as comfortable as you can."

He closed the door linking the front office with the cells behind. Hawk watched the heavy oak planks swing into place, cutting off much of the light, and turned to study his cell.

It was a block of stone-encrusted vacuum, ten by ten by ten. The side and rear walls, and the ceiling, were concreted stone. High up on the rear wall there was a narrow window with half-inch bars set deep and solid into the sill. The fourth wall was barred, a cage that had just one five-foot door, a two-by-one grate at the foot hinged so that food might be passed in. There was a bunk bolted against one wall, two chains holding it in place. It was covered with a striped palliasse and a grey blanket. There was a plain cotton pillow. Underneath the bunk there was a slop bucket and a jug of water. Otherwise the cell was empty, except for the graffiti scratched into the walls.

Hawk sat down on the bunk and watched the sun dance thin rays of light through the window. He rubbed absently at his gloved left hand, fighting the claustrophobia that was starting to climb up his spine and take a grip, like spider's mandibles, on his mind. He had been in jail once before. Just the one time. Just long enough to know he hated it.

Couldn't take it. Not without going mad.

He rubbed at the glove and thought back . . .

Tularosa . . .

A hot morning that turned into a hotter afternoon . . .

A cell . . . And the threat of death . . .

A judge had come in then, a circuit rider more attuned to giving the attentive crowd the spectacle they hoped to see than he was to dispensing real justice. It had been understood between the judge and the sheriff that Hawk would hang anyway. The fact of his employer's hiring of an Eastern lawyer was an annoyance that served only to spin the trial out and leave the young man sweating in the cell.

Learning to mistrust lawmen and judges and courts. Learning to hate them.

And learning to feel nervous when four walls and a locked door confined him.

He had escaped then. Escaped with the hood fastened over his face and the rope chafing his neck. Escaped with all hope gone, and only an empty pit of fear and hate left inside him.

John T. McLain had sprung him— almost literally—from the final descent into darkness. He had produced a pardon that got the rope lifted from Jared's neck; the hood taken from his face.

It had left the young gunfighter with three immutable impressions. One was a deep mistrust of the law: the conviction that justice was personal, and too many appointed officers ready to take bribes. The second was a firm friendship with John T. McLain: the knowledge that a man could win friends who would stand by him, no matter what; so long as he proved himself worthy of their trust. The third thing was a deep-seated fear of confined spaces.

The long weeks spent in the cell. The hot, breath-stifling hood. The rope around his neck. All had come together to terrify him of confinement.

He had sworn then, riding clear of the Tularosa gallows, that he would never submit to that awful confinement again.

And he never had. Until now . . .

He stood up, feeling the walls closing down; feeling the heat and the sour smell of sweat and stale urine and despairing hopes trample in around him. He went over to the window. Tried to reach up high enough that he could lift his body from the floor and look out into the open. But the sill was too deep and he couldn't fasten his hands on the bars.

He paced over to the front wall and thrust his arms out through the cage. A warm breeze wafted the corridor, carrying the stink of sour vomit from the adjoining cell, drifting through the dusty, dim air like a threat; or a promise of disgust to come.

He backed away and began to study the scratchings on the walls. That at least took his mind off his confinement.

There was one that said: *I never raped her. She asked for money.* Beneath it,

someone else had inscribed *Golden balls.*
Another said: *1876 is a bad year. I don't
like hanging around.*

None of them made him feel any better
and he settled on the bunk, tilting his hat
over his face and closing his eyes in an
attempt to shut out the blank emptiness of
the walls, to shut out the impressing facts
of his imprisonment.

Around noon, the door connecting the
cells to the outer office opened and a
deputy came through with a tray of food.

"You're doin' pretty good, feller," he
said. "Mister Parmalee got special orders
fer you."

Hawk took the tray from the grating
and carried it over to the bunk.

"He got me out yet?" he asked.

The deputy shook his head, grinning.
"Don't think even ole Ben can do that,
feller. Stoker's got his mind fixed to hold
you here until the judge arrives. Funny,
that. Buford Stoker's a Parmalee man. Got
hisself elected fer that selfsame reason, but
now he's all law-an'-order. Ain't listenin'

to Parmalee at all. Just insists on holdin'
you until Judge Walker arrives."

He turned away, pausing at the outer
door.

"Don't envy you, feller. Judge Walker's
a hangman. An' he takes his time on every
case. Be weeks before he gets up to Green
Springs"

"Thanks," said Hawk. "Thanks a lot."

"My pleasure," said the deputy. "Yore
loss."

And shut the door.

Hawk sat down on the bunk and lifted the
cloth from the tray. There was a plate with
a big steak surrounded by potatoes and
hash greens. A bowl full of biscuits and
another with a thick slice of apple pie. A
pot of coffee and a smaller mug of cream
flanked the main courses.

He began to eat.

He was halfway through the steak when
his fork sank into the mashed potato and
grated on something hard. He wiped the
implement against the edge of the plate
and saw a shiny sliver of metal fall loose

from the prongs. When he fetched it loose from the smearing of food he found a thin cylinder of foil, rolled up like a cartridge.

He opened it, unfolding a thin streamer of silver that held inside it a narrow sheet of paper. There was a brief message written on the paper: *Dawn tomorrow. Be ready.*

There was no signature.

Hawk crumpled the silver foil and lobbed the wad out through the window. Then he chewed the paper to a sticky wet strip and spat it into the bucket beneath his bunk. He finished his meal and shoved the empty dishes out through the grate. Climbed on to the bunk and closed his eyes.

The cell was dark when Stoker opened the door and danced a kerosene lantern across the frontages of the cages.

"Sleep well," he said. "You may as well get used to it."

"Yeah," Hawk replied. "I guess so."

The light went away behind the fat peace officer, and the door snapped closed. A bolt slid into place and there was silence.

The cells were not lit. The only illumination came from the underside of the outer door: a thin line of faint yellow light that did little except spread a dim swathe of half-invisible radiance across no more than four feet of stone floor. It was just enough that Hawk could see the fat-bellied spiders scuttling across the stones to the remnants of dropped food, and the darker shapes of cockroaches trying to get there first.

He climbed up on the bunk and closed his eyes, trying to ignore the insects that scurried over his body as he waited for the dawn.

It was a long night, and sleepless. Anticipation and disgust and claustrophobia mingling together to produce a restless mixture of hope and sleep.

Dawn found him open-eyed, watching a spider crawl leisurely over the ceiling of his cell as the first darts of the early light glanced radiance over the stone, lighting up the scrabbling arachnid and his hopes.

He used the slop bucket and then splashed water from the jug over his face and hands, used the blanket to towel dry. And waited. Green Springs was silent, false dawn giving way to that period of grey stillness that precedes the sun's true rising. The air was chill, faint tendrils of mist creeping in through the window, ghostly in the dim light. Hawk went over to the front of the cell and gripped the bars in both hands.

The outer office was quiet except for the stertorous rumblings of a sleeping deputy. Hawk wondered what was going to happen. If anything would happen.

Then there was the faint click of a catch turning, a squeak of unoiled hinges. The deputy's snoring ceased and there was the thud of boots hitting bare wood, a rattle of springs. A muffled voice said, "Hold it!" And boots drummed louder on the planks. A man cried out once, softly, and there was the protest of springs as some heavy object crashed down on to the bed.

The door opened and a man stepped through. He wore a shapeless duster and his head was hidden beneath a black cotton sack. Only his piercing blue eyes were visible through the holes cut in the cotton. He held a converted Colt's Navy model in his left hand: in his right were the keys.

He opened the cell door and waved Hawk through to the outer office.

Two men waited there, dressed in the same concealing disguise, with Colt Peacemakers in their hands. Hawk said, "Thanks," and stepped over to the gun rack fastened against the wall. He located his belt and buckled it around his waist, then lifted the Meteor clear and loaded the shotgun. His Colt was on a shelf, the cylinder emptied: he reloaded the pistol on five chambers and dropped it into the holster.

"Can we get goin', fer Chrissakes!" grumbled one of the masked men. "I don't wanta be here when Stoker comes in."

"He'll be late." Hawk recognized Parmalee's voice. "I got him good an' drunk last night."

"Where're my saddlebags?" Hawk demanded. "You know?"

"Try the cupboard." Parmalee gestured

at a box built into the wall behind the desk. "But hurry."

Hawk opened the cupboard and lifted his saddlebags out. His money was still intact, so he slung the bags over his left shoulder and moved towards the door. On the bed, the deputy groaned. He was resting on his side with his wrists lashed together and his legs drawn up at right angles where the bonds securing his ankles were fastened to his hands. A bandanna gagged his mouth, and where his short-cropped hair exposed the pale skin behind the right ear, an ugly purple bruise was forming.

"Yore horse is outside," said Parmalee. "Let's go."

The other two went out to the street with obvious relief. Hawk followed them, slipping his bags behind the saddle and lifting astride the black horse as Parmalee closed the door. As soon as the mine owner was mounted, all four men took off down the street at a fast canter.

The mist was beginning to disperse, and lights were shining from the windows of the houses and stores, smoke lifting in lazy spirals through the silent air. A cat shrieked irritably as their passage disturbed its scavenging, and from a neighbouring building a dog began to bark furiously. They rode the full length of the main street, passing only a single figure: the black-robed shape of Father Durant plodding bleary-eyed to the church to prepare for the early service.

Hawk glanced at the priest and realized it was Sunday, then the lonely figure was gone into the mist behind them and they were riding away from Green Springs along the northern trail.

Two miles outside of town Parmalee called a halt and tugged the mask clear of his head. The others followed suit, stripping out of their dusters and rolling the coats into tight balls that they stowed behind their saddles.

"We'll burn 'em when we get to the mine," said Parmalee. "An' if anyone should ask you—you was both on guard all night."

They nodded, grinning now that the

158

immediate danger was gone and the full force of the excitement hit them. One was a boy, no older than Hawk had been when he first took up the gun. His face was smooth and blandly handsome, barely touched by the first shadings of stubble. He wore a green shirt and snug-fitting denim pants with a cutaway holster tied down on the right thigh.

His eyes were dark as his skin, and smiling as he said, "Ain't had so much fun since we hurrawed that saloon in Waco."

The other man was older, around his mid-thirties, with stringy hair and a mustache to match. His eyes were brown, and cold under the excitement.

"That was a saloon, Billy. This time it's a sheriff's office. Stoker ever catches us, we go down fer a long time."

"He ain't gonna catch us," grinned the kid. "Is he, mister Parmalee?"

He reminded Hawk of a man he had known in Texas. A young man called John Wesley Hardin.

"Not if we're careful, boy," said the mine owner. "Not so long as you remember to cover yore trail an' not shoot yore mouth off. You heed Ben—he knows what he talks about."

Ben grunted and fetched a hunk of chewing tobacco from his vest. Hawk recognized in him the signs of a professional. He said, "Thanks. I appreciate what you done."

Billy grinned and shrugged. Ben spat a wiry strand of tobacco on to the grass and said, "Weren't fer you, feller. Did that fer the boss."

Parmalee said, "Let's leave the reception party an' get the hell outta here."

He turned his pony eastwards, cutting through the dew-wet grass until they reached a narrow stream that was flanked by willows and aspens. He led the way into the water and walked the animal a quarter mile up the valley. Then he took them out on to an area of hard rock and turned north again. They crossed the rock and left a trail over a wide meadow filled with lush grass and sunflowers that ended abruptly on the rim of a shallow ravine. They went down the bank and up the other side, cutting into a second area of grass. This covered a quarter mile or more before a fresh stream bisected the green, flowing down to cut across the main northern trail. Parmalee swung his horse round in midstream and began to ride east again, heading for the ridge of hills bordering the farthest perimeter of the valley.

"If Stoker gets a posse up," he said, "he'll likely think we went north. Tried to hide our trail until we could cut back to the main roadway."

"Where are we going?" asked Hawk. "What you got in mind?"

"Simple," said Parmalee. "We're headin' for the mine. So far as Stoker's concerned, Billy an' Ben been on guard all night. Me, after I was drinkin' with that goddam fat-gut useless lawman, I went up to the cabin I got there. I was sleepin' off a hangover."

The stream got steeper and rougher and their horses slowed to a dragging walk, fighting the current and the cold. A mile up, Parmalee took them out on to a wide fan of shale that took some hard climbing, but scattered behind them to hide any hoofprints. After that, they were on bedrock, hard and hot in the growing heat, and incapable of recording any tracks. They followed it up along the flank of the hills and then turned through a narrow split on to a wider trail that led directly to the rimrock.

Parmalee took them up until they were looking down over the valley. Green Springs was a faint shape in the distance. They followed the line of the rimrock along until the trail descended in a sweeping curve to a high valley that was cut like a slice of cake from the main body of the Jornado range.

The air here stank of metal and heat and sweat, and the mist that had dissipated from the lowlands was reinforced by the smouldering fumes lifting from the huts below. The apex of the vee-shape formed by the cut was riddled with holes that burst from the rock like the openings in a maggoty apple. Each one was fronted by a timber platform that fed narrow-gauge rail tracks down to a secondary catchment area, where there were sheds and bunkers into which the raw ore was tipped. A network of tracks connected each hole to a series of six sheds, larger than the others, and giving off a hot, sickly smell. After those there was a further linkage that connected all the sheds to a terminal where loading bays were built, with stables and bunkhouses for the miners and the guards.

On the western edge of the valley, where the tall phalanxes of rock fell down over the main descent, there was a high, solid-looking fence. It spanned the entire edge of the rim, open in two places where gates had been let in, that opened on to the trails leading down to Green Springs.

Over to one side, built on a miniature plateau that jutted out from the southern wall, there was a cabin.

Parmalee tossed his duster and mask to Ben and said, "Burn it all." Then he led Hawk up the steep path towards the cabin.

Inside it was sparsely comfortable. There was a large room with Indian blankets covering the scrubbed planks of the floor. A large fireplace with four chairs facing it, and a glass-fronted liquor cabinet behind them. There was a small kitchen and two bedrooms built into the natural rock. It was warm and lonely: the habitation of a solitary man.

"You still ready to go down to Las Cruces?" Parmalee forked eggs and bacon on to Hawk's plate. "There ain't too long before the end o' the month."

"Long enough," said the gunfighter. "I can make it."

"Then what?" The old man slumped into a chair and began to eat. "This thing about Johanna sayin' I sent her worries me."

"There's two things in your favour," said Hawk. "Someone sent her to me. It wasn't to kill me, or she'd have done that while I was asleep. So it has to be that she was sent to find out what I knew about the gold."

He shrugged, remembering what the girl felt like. Remembering, too, the bloody vision of her body collapsing through the window.

"She never had time to find out much. So whoever sent her, still doesn't know. Brava and Vansittart aren't likely to trust one another enough that they'll forget that wagon in Las Cruces, nor chance a split without both of them being there. So I go down to the canyon and take the wagon out. Then I come up to Blanco and wait. That way, I should lead the informer into a trap."

"On yore own?" said Parmalee. "With maybe two teams?"

"Send some men with me," said Hawk. "Two good men."

"Billy an' Ben," said Parmalee. "Wouldn't hurt fer them to be outta town fer a spell."

Hawk nodded, "All right. Fetch them."

They quit the rimrock in a line. Ben Galant at the front, Hawk at centre, Billy Garrett riding tail. It was close on noon, and the heat was shifting the miasma of smoke in a lung-clogging haze up from Parmalee's sheds. Hawk wound a bandanna over his face and rode with his head slumped on to his chest, trusting the black horse to follow Ben's grey pony. They followed the rimrock along to the southern curve of the valley surrounding Green Springs, then cut west and east, tailing down over the swing of land to pick up the southern trail.

When the stink of the mines cleared out of the air, Hawk lifted his bandanna from his face.

"You don't like this, do you?" he called.

Billy laughed, and said, "Best fun I had since we bust Stoker's office. I'm enjoying it real fine."

Ben turned round in his saddle and spat a long streamer of tobacco on to the grass.

"You think you're something special, Hawk. Me, I'm just a man doin' a job on account o' my boss told me to. An' he's the man payin' the wages. I'd put you where you belong: feedin' worms inside a coffin, or payin' time in a cell. I'm doin' this because Ben Parmalee told me to."

Hawk grinned. "You with the bunch that got jumped by Brava, Ben?"

"No." Galant shook his head. "My brother was. Why?"

"Sounds like you're sour about it," said Hawk. "Besides, you took work with Parmalee that you knew wasn't nothing more'n toting a gun. How's that make you so different?"

"I just work fer mister Parmalee," said Ben. "He pays me a regular wage an' I do my job."

"Which includes gunning the odd robber," said Hawk. "When you can hit him. And bustin' people outta jail. Where's the difference?"

"Depends on how you look at it," said Galant. "I got a steady contract an' a bed at night I know I can go home to. You, all you've got is a gun an' a horse."

"How much do you make, Ben?" Hawk's voice got low and cold. "What's Parmalee pay you for this contract? How much d'you make a month?"

"That ain't yore business," said Galant. "I know where I'm well off."

"Yeah," said Hawk, "I guess that means a lot to you. To most people. Me, I go to where I want. I live the way I like an' I don't let anyone tell me what to do."

"You got a big mouth," said Ben. "You needed us to bust you outta jail."

"Sure," said Hawk, "but you did it. Just goes to show."

"What?" Ben asked. "What's it show?"

"You listened," Hawk said quietly. "And you did it. You think about that."

9

LAS CRUCES was built close against the Rio Grande on the old Comanche Trail. It hung in a series of terraces from the high flanks of the surrounding mountains, adobe houses folding down like giant building blocks to the flatter ground along the river. In the noonday sunlight the adobe shone blindingly white, contrasting with the roseate sand of the cliffs and the greenish-blue of the fast-flowing river.

It was a large town, bigger than Green Springs or Cabanos, with two saloons and two hotels. Even a wharf built out into the water. There was a bank and a church and a sheriff's office and down at one end of the street closest to the water, there was a two-storey wooden building separated from the others, with red lanterns hung along the frontage.

"I'm hungry," Billy complained. "We gonna get some decent food now?"

Hawk studied the town: it looked quiet. Then he twisted in his saddle, standing upright in the stirrups to scan their backtrail. There was no sign of pursuit, so he said:

"All right. Don't look like Stoker sent anyone after us. We'll go in an' get something to eat. We need supplies, anyway."

"Best we find the canyon," said Ben Galant. "Fetch that wagon out afore them outlaws shift it."

Hawk shrugged. "You know what day of the month it is?"

Ben shook his head. "Ain't rightly sure. Close to payday, that I know."

Billy grinned as Hawk took a sheet of crumpled paper from his vest and began to study the markings.

"I took a calendar from Parmalee," said the gunfighter. "I been marking off the days from when we left the mine. Braco said they was due to meet at the end o' the month. That gives us maybe three days either side. It's the twenty-sixth now, so

I reckon we got time to eat. Besides, we could be in for a long, hungry wait."

"What month is it, anyway?" asked Ben; still frowning. "I clear forgot."

"September," said Hawk. "All mist an' mellow an' golden."

Ben spat and followed the gunfighter down the trail into Las Cruces.

They ate in one of the saloons, sharing a bottle of whisky between them. The liquor mellowed Ben enough that his initial mistrust of Hawk gave way to a grudging confidence. Billy just ate, mostly ignoring the whisky as he listened to the two older men talking.

"What we doin' next?" Ben asked, accepting Hawk's leadership.

"We buy supplies an' go find that canyon," murmured the gunfighter, spooning gravy into his mouth. "Then we wait."

"I don't get it," grumbled Ben. "Why not just take the wagon?"

"We'll do that," Hawk answered calmly. "Soon as we got the supplies."

"So where's the waitin' come in?" Ben topped their glasses. "I don't figger that part."

"How many men you think it'll need to take that wagon back to Parmalee?" asked Hawk.

Ben swallowed liquor and said, "One good man. Them outlaws only had four to handle three loads, an' they was running."

"What I reckoned," Hawk agreed. "So one o' you gets to drive a wagonload of gold back to your boss."

Billy chuckled and said, "Suppose we run off with it? What then?"

"You get hunted down an' killed." Hawk's voice was cold enough, and his grey eyes hard enough that the youngster began to choke on his food. "I come after you."

"Ain't no one gonna run off with it," said Ben. "But what do the other two do?"

"Wait," said Hawk. "Like I said. We take the wagon out with one man driving. Then me an' the second man wait around for Brava an' Vansittart to show up. When they see the wagon's off an' gone, they're gonna do one of two things. Either they decide it got lifted by their *compadres,* or they reckon it got found. That leaves them two choices: head down to Calaveros in hopes of finding the other two, or cut their losses an' fetch the last wagon out of Blanco Canyon."

Ben nodded: "Makes sense, but what then?"

"If they go south," said Hawk, "I'll follow them. I reckon they'd go north, though. Pick up the last wagon an' forget about the feller told them about the shipment. Just take it out an' leave him. Shit! He ain't about to start complaining overloud."

He lifted his glass and emptied it. Filled it again.

"Still leaves two of us waitin' inside the canyon," said Ben.

"One in, one out," Hawk corrected. "Whatever happens, the man outside goes back to Green Springs. If they head north, he can side the wagon driver with me coming up behind. If they head south, he helps shift the wagon while I go after them."

"You want the glory, I guess," said Ben. "Keep it all to yourself."

"No," Hawk said. "I just want to kill them."

They finished eating and went out to buy supplies. Each man stocked up with enough to last him through a week of hard living: just enough that he could stay alive from the sacks slung behind his saddle. Then they rode out of town and moved towards the canyon.

Like Charley Braco had said, it was five miles north of Las Cruces: set up high on a secondary trail that took them the remainder of the day to find. The trail was no more than a ledge running along the flank of the cliffs, barely wide enough to allow a wagon to pass, and the canyon was even more difficult. The entrance was a thin split in the rock, wider at the base than at the top, where the walls seemed to lean together, the curling roots of piñon and wild cedar joining to form a shadowy roof. Brava's men had cut the original scrub away and then dragged it back in place all along the thirty-foot gap.

Hawk and Billy and Ben spent close on an hour clearing it before they were able to lead their horses into the canyon itself.

By the time they got inside, the sun was going down. Shining clear and bright like the focused glare of a magnifying glass into the entrance of a huge cavern that was hung with long-dried skins and older skulls. Tiers of hand-cut steps lifted on either side of the hole, ceremonial entrances to the ancient burial cave. The rock was covered with paint, buffalo and antelope and horses mingling with the stylized stick figures of Indians, coyotes, emblems of the moon and sun. There was an air of stillness in the place, not entirely compounded of the high walls and overhanging trees. Rather, it was a product of age and veneration; of holiness that was ruptured and defiled by the entrance of unbelievers.

"It's goddam creepy," said Billy. "Like a fuckin' graveyard."

He was right: the place was a graveyard. All around the walls of the small canyon, all around the caves that opened cleaner than the mouths of Ben Parmalee's mines, there were skulls hung. Horse bones, and those of wolves and coyotes and foxes. Those of men. They shone yellow in the light that was reflected off the walls, scoured by the wind and the rain and the sun that had withered the shields and banners and clothes set beside them to wispy tatters. The high walls kept the light flickering into shadow dancing over the three men, and magnified their voices so that they seemed to echo like the calling of ghosts from the sullen caves, the blank eyes of the rock that stared down at them.

Then the strident cry of a hungry mule broke the pall of awed whispers. It rang, high and screeching around the box canyon, coming from the cave beneath the main fissure.

"They must be hungry," said Hawk. "An' if Brava kept them here, he must be close enough to feed them. Let's get them out."

They went down to the far end of the canyon.

The unhappy mules were penned inside the smaller cave Charley Braco had described to Hawk. They were hobbled behind a rough barrier of cholla and ropes. Ben produced a knife and hacked through the spread lariats, then all three men kicked the cholla clear and brought the mules out into the open.

Behind them, inside a cave that was hung with skulls and the mouldering remnants of long-dead Indians, there was a single wagon. A Studebaker, the wheels greased, the bed covered with the same thick tarpaulin Hawk had seen in Calaveros.

They hitched their own horses to the traces to drag it out, and when they lifted the rear flaps of the tarpaulin cover they saw the dull, tempting gleam of gold ingots.

The sun was going down fast now, splitting the box canyon into shadows and threatening to obscure the trail out. They hitched the mules into the harness and eased the Studebaker carefully—slowly— out on to the trail. Then they brought their own ponies out and set the brush back in place through the entrance. By then it was twilight.

"Who takes the wagon?" Hawk asked. "Who's the best driver?"

"Billy," said Ben. "Ain't no doubt."

"Aw, shit!" grumbled Billy. "I wanta stay around. See what happens when them outlaws turn up."

"We'll tell you," said Hawk. "Get that goddam load up to Green Springs."

Ben hitched the kid's horse to the tailgate and ruminated a smile.

"You get it done, boy. I'll see you back there."

Billy climbed on to the wagon and lifted the mules to a clopping trot: "I hope so," he said. "I surely hope so."

Hawk and Ben Galant took their ponies down the trail to where a fan of tree-covered land lifted eastwards of the canyon. Ben tethered his inside a thicket of aspens fifty yards off the trail. Hawk took the black horse higher up, hobbling it close to the rimrock. Then he climbed back down to where Ben was waiting.

The older man took up position inside the trees overlooking the trail. Hawk climbed back to the rimrock. That way he could see the entrance to the box canyon and both sides of the exit trail; Ben could only see the way north.

It was a long, cold night without a fire but that might have alerted Brava and Vansittart. Hawk ate beans cold and chewed on a chunk of pemmican with his saddle blanket wrapped around his shoulders as he watched the canyon get dark and the stars come up.

The sky was clear, a deep velvet blue that was pin-pricked with dots of silver. Slowly—though he realized that its slowness was largely due to his waiting—a thin sliver of moon lifted over the sky. It was pale and scarcely bright enough to shed light over the ground, only a few days clear of its waning.

It reminded him of a time he had waited out with Hickok . . .

A long time ago, or so it felt . . .

Up on a bluff west of Abilene . . .

Waiting for five wanted men to pass along the trail below . . .

Hickok had stayed up on the high ground, carefully checking the cartridges he spread out in a neat line, ready to snap into the breech of his Sharps buffalo gun. He had sent Jared down to cover the lower part of the trail. And when the young deputy had asked about that, querying his own proximity to the prospective outlaws, Hickok had said:

"I know what I can do. I got me a Sharps in .50 calibre, an' I know I can hit the men I see. That carbine you're carryin' don't throw even near half the range. An' I can't be sure you shoot so straight I want to risk bein' close to you. You go on down. If you hit two of them before I do, I'll side you next time around."

He had. Because when the outlaws showed up, Jared sighted on the lead rider and blew half his belly out over the rump of his stolen pony. Then he levered the carbine across and over and took out the left eye of the second man with a lucky shot. He was aiming at the belly, but the horse had bucked and lifted the man high up in the saddle so that he slumped forwards as the pony landed back on the ground, almost falling from the saddle, then falling all the way as his skull got mashed up by the bullet.

The other three had concentrated their fire on the position they could see: Jared's. He had ducked down and listened to the slugs ricochet around him, holding low to the rocks as he felt splinters burst over his face and waited for a chance bullet to find a target.

He hadn't even heard the heavy thunder of Wild Bill's buffalo gun, just stayed crouched down until all the firing ceased. Then he had stood up and seen three men, the last of the outlaws, spread over the moonlit ground. All dead. All with neat chest shots spreading their lifeblood over the sand.

After a while, Hickok had clambered down and said, "That's what I mean. You did good taking two out, but the other three would've hit you had I not been up there. That's worth rememberin': if you get allowed a choice, take the high ground every time. That way, you stay alive longer."

Hawk had long remembered.

Long enough to stay alive . . . Long enough to place Ben Galant down below . . .

Night faded into day. The clarity of the stars gave way to the indistinct greyness of the dawn mists. Off to the east the sun fought a few rays of reddish-gold light through the blankness, lighting up the top of the sky so that the last vestiges of night got lit with a radiance that dulled out the stars without illuminating the ground beneath. Birds began to sing, and small animals crept from their burrows and holes to sniff cautiously at the new day. Then a wind got up out of the east and began to blow the fog away over the tops of the cliffs and a single, massive shine of light struck through all the greyness so that the farther valleys of the Rio Grande were bright with a multitude of iridescent colours.

Hawk shivered and began to chew on a piece of cold meat, watching the land below.

Dawn gave way to morning. Cool stillness became noisy heat as the sun rose and warmed the rimrock. Squirrels chattered angrily at the silent man who chewed and ignored them. A skunk wandered languorously across the ground in front of him, tail raised high in preparation of defence, then disappeared amongst the trees without cause to disturb the watcher. He saw two foxes race like red ghosts amongst the aspens; watched a badger stumble back to its set, jaws bloody with the remains of the night's prey.

And then saw two riders negotiate the trail up to the box canyon.

Instantly, he was alert. The Winchester

came up into his hands like a faithful dog ready for action. The sound of the lever clicking back and then up was lost under the muffling bulk of the trees.

They halted at the mouth of the canyon. Dismounted. And began to drag the brushwood away from the entrance. So far they were indistinct shadows under the overhang of the cliffs, features and clothing mostly lost beneath the shadow. It was not until they had all the brushwood dragged out and led their horses inside the canyon that Hawk was able to recognize them clearly as Luis Brava and Cole Vansittart.

He waited, stretched flat over the upper lip of the canyon, as they ran towards the cave at the farther end. Waited for them to come out screaming like the wind and head back to their horses.

He grinned, enjoying their panic, and moved towards his own mount.

He got up in the saddle and steered the black horse along the rimrock to where he could see them come out from the canyon and choose their direction.

They went north. Along the high trail that led to Green Springs.

Hawk slammed his heels against the sides of the black horse and took the animal down the slope at a speed that was faster than safe. He was halfway down, sliding over the shale with the pony's hindquarters dug deep into the loose rock and the forefeet stuck out in front without any attempt to control its direction when the shots rang out.

Luis Brava and Cole Vansittart had run back from the empty cave without either man trusting the other. Their main aim was to get back to their horses and find out where the wagon had gone before either one got a lead on what might be a doublecross.

They mounted up and turned to face one another, both settling hands close to their guns.

"Charley an' Wade went to Calaveros," snarled Vansittart. "That's Mexican country, Luis. You set somethin' up with them?"

"The other wagon's your side of the border," snapped Brava. "Maybe you arranged for your friend in Green Springs to take this one, so you'd have two to share."

"No." Vansittart shook his head. "I never told no one else about this one."

"So where's your *amigo* Charley?" snarled Brava. "Your *compadre* Wade?"

"They was in Calaveros," said the Southerner. "They should be here by now. They knew the date."

"They aren't," said Brava; simply. "They aren't here and the wagon is gone. That leaves us a problem, *amigo*."

The last word came out slow and ugly. Vansittart recognized the threat implicit in the voice and shrugged.

"We still got one. Let's go fetch that. Forget the other feller an' take it south. Maybe we'll catch up with whoever took the second one."

"*Bueno*," said Brava. "*Vamanos!*"

They took off along the trail leading north. Neither man was fully sure that the

186

other wasn't lying, so both kept their hands close to their guns.

Then, where the curve of the trail began to slope down on to the main route, Ben Galant stepped out in front of them. He was holding a Winchester carbine across his chest and his mouth was empty of tobacco as he got ready to stop the outlaws who had taken his boss's gold. Ready, also, to prove that he could do better than some hired-in gunfighter like Hawk.

He had the Winchester cocked and his right forefinger was tight on the trigger.

He was ready for trouble. Ready to prove himself.

The trouble was, he wasn't quite ready enough for two hardcase killers like Brava and Vansittart.

"Stop!" he yelled, bringing the Winchester up to his shoulder. "I'll kill you else!"

Neither man stopped. Brava just drew the Colt holstered on his left hip and began to trigger bullets into the man standing at the centre of the trail as he rode his horse headlong into the obstacle. Beside him, swinging to the side, Vansittart lifted the S&W Schofield from under his left arm and planted three neat shots into Ben Galant's belly and chest.

Brava's bullets served to turn the aim of the Winchester, blowing wild around Galant's chest and face. One plucked the lobe of the man's ear away as he triggered the carbine and swung the muzzle between the two charging horsemen, undecided as to which target he should take out first.

It was the last mistake he ever made.

The slug that took away the lobe of his left ear caused him to scream and turn in that direction. The movement exposed his right side to the following bullets, tracking his carbine out of line with a second shot wasted into the trees.

Luis Brava's next shot went in through his ribs, hitting low on the exposed right side to shatter bone and deflect upwards into the lung. At the same time as Ben Galant pitched backwards under the impact of the shot, Cole Vansittart's first bullet slammed into his body. It hit against the shield of bone protecting Ben's chest, fracturing it and embedding under the muscle. The second caught him as he twisted round. It entered his belly where the material of his vest was separated by his backwards movement from his pants. It tore through the muscle and drove into the softer membranes beneath, opening up a wide hole through which gouted a spurt of blood and half-digested food and whisky. The third hit higher up, going in just beneath the apex of the ribcage so that it tore away the centre of Ben Galant's stomach and spilled most of it out behind him.

His body was caught in the crossfire, Vansittart's shots killing him as Brava pumped wild lead around his plunging body.

A slug entered the skull, going in through the stretched skin of the open, screaming jaws to shatter teeth and dance upwards in horrible parody of butterfly movement against bones and nerves and teeth. It ricocheted off of Galant's hind-ward molars and ploughed up through the roof of his mouth into his neck. Blood exploded from his mouth as it glanced off and tore through the delicate tendrils of nerves that connected his ears and eyes to his brain.

He was suddenly deaf. And blind. And all he knew was pain.

And then it ended as the slug hit his brain and blanked out everything. Like a great curtain sliding down across his mind, leaving nothing for anyone to see in front and nothing behind except the bare, dark shadows of death; of non-existence: only darkness.

Luis Brava and Cole Vansittart rode their horses across his body and laughed as it crumpled and collapsed under the hooves. Like a bag folding, crushed and shattered under careless hands.

They rode away, moving south.

Hawk followed after them.

He came down off the rimrock and cursed Ben Galant's mangled body for doing the wrong thing. He reined in long enough to free the nervous grey pony from its place amongst the trees, and then took off after Brava and Vansittart.

The body didn't bother him much: he had seen corpses as bad, and Ben wasn't a friend, anyway. In Hawk's estimation he was just an over-tired gunfighter looking to make a reputation with his boss. Which meant he was too old and too slow to do his work properly. Had he been sensible about it, he would have shot the two riders from the cover of the trees. Had he done what Hawk asked him, he would have stayed back and let them go past so that two men might have trailed them back to Green Springs.

Now there was only one. And Billy Garrett riding the wagon: a raw kid with a tired team and a heavy load. And two murderous outlaws chasing him all the way along the road.

Hawk heeled the black horse into a canter that took them fast up the trail.

He wasn't sure if he was hurrying to save Billy Garrett or the gold, or just to kill Luis Brava and Cole Vansittart. It didn't really matter: he had made a promise to

Ben Parmalee, and—more important—to himself. And Jared Hawk was a man who kept his promises.

Especially when they involved his chosen trade.

Especially when they involved death.

10

BILLY GARRETT held the mules to a steady pace throughout the night, steering by the moon along the narrow trail until he was able to descend to the broader roadway of the main path. The going was easier there, but he didn't lift the pace any, preferring to maintain a regular speed that would leave the animals with reserves of strength should a fast dash be called for. He felt disgruntled that Ben and Hawk had detailed him to handle the wagon: he had wanted to be around the canyon when the outlaws arrived, maybe join in the fighting if it came to that.

Billy enjoyed fighting. The thrill of danger gave him a lift that he couldn't find anywhere else. Not in liquor or women or even the peyote he had tried chewing one time in Mexico. He was nineteen years old and had killed two men to his certain knowledge. One—the first—was a rustler he had shot while riding herd on a bunch of Texas longhorns. The man had come sneaking up in the night while most of the drovers were whooping it up in Amarillo, thinking to cut out a few head without the sleepy night guards spotting him. Billy had. And had shot him down with only two bullets. The second killing was a year later, when Billy was eighteen. He had been playing cards in a dirty little saloon in Galenas; losing money. Then realizing that he was losing because the man handling the deck was a cardsharp. Billy had called him out, and when the gambler produced a derringer, the young cowboy had drawn his Colt and put three bullets into the man's chest. The mayor of Galenas, who was also the peace officer, had suggested it might be better for Billy's health if he left town, so the boy drifted south. Worked for a spell as a bank guard in Fronteras, then signed on with a cattle drive going up to Albuquerque. The Parmalee stage line was taking on men there, and Billy had become a shotgun rider. Three times he had fought off attacks on his coach, and though he didn't claim it, he was pretty sure he had killed at least one more man. That was how Ben Parmalee had noticed him and promoted him to the better-paid position of mine guard.

The thought cheered Billy.

If he was the one brought the gold back to Green Springs, then the boss was certain to be pleased. It would be quite something, and even allowing that Hawk was planning the whole thing and it was still him and Ben back at the canyon, it would be Billy who brought the wagon in.

He began to whistle tunelessly, thinking about the bonus he might get as the sun came up and began to clear the clouds from the high walls surrounding the river.

When it was full light he halted and fed the animals, digging out a can of preserves and some hardtack for himself. When he was finished he tossed the can into the river and watched it bob away downstream. He was tempted to shoot at it, but decided that wasn't the kind of thing a real gunman would do. Not a professional like Hawk. So instead he checked the animals and climbed back into the seat of the Studebaker and moved on northwards.

The mules were tired now, despite the halt, and the pace slowed down to a plodding walk. The trail ran wide and flat alongside the river, high cliffs shining gold in the sunlight on both sides. They held in the heat, filling the long split with sleepy warmth, the plodding of the mules adding a somnolent rocking motion to the wagon.

Billy's eyes got heavy and his head drooped, chin resting against his chest. He allowed himself to doze the way cowboys do on a drive: limbs relaxing and senses dulling without ever quite falling all the way asleep. He was aware of the wagon's forwards motion, of the heat and the drowsy murmuring of the river, and every so often he turned his head slowly from side to side, listening for the sound of hoofbeats behind him.

Morning turned into noonday and the sun got higher and hotter. The trail began to skirt up from the river valley on a curving line that brought it, finally, back to the high ground. Billy halted where the path opened on a wide meadow and allowed the panting mules to rest again, cropping the lush grass. To the east, a curving fan of land slanted down to the meadow, the slope covered with a dense confusion of pines and aspens. The silvery trees got lost behind him, giving way to the hardier conifers that flourished in the broken country to the south. To the north, where the trail bled out of the meadow, there was a thinner stand of timber, a stream cutting down the length of a ravine to the now-distant waters of the Rio Grande. Sunflowers and poppies grew in the meadow, the brightness of their yellow and red flowers contrasting brilliantly with the emerald green of the grass.

Billy sipped water and stretched back against the wagon's forward wheel as he chose food from his sack. He felt warm and safe and comfortable.

The high trail split where a natural fold in the land opened a gap on to the river. To the west, leading down to the bank of the Rio Grande, there was a steadily widening path that ran down in a gentle slant to the side of the water. From there, the trail went off to the north and south, wide enough that two wagons might pass abreast. The higher trail continued narrow and tree-lined, running arrow-straight for the gap. On the rim it curved eastwards, running alongside the ravine until the declivity got narrow enough that a man might slide his horse down the southern patch and then climb up the northern bank to rejoin the trail farther along where it came out into a stand of timber.

Luis Brava and Cole Vansittart halted their ponies there and began to talk about their next move

"If the wagon's goin' north, then it has to take the bottom trail." Vansittart pointed at the higher ground. "There ain't no way you could bring a wagon over that."

"It's the fastest road to Blanco Canyon," said Brava. "A man on a horse could reach it inside three days."

"Man with a wagon couldn't reach it at all," grunted the American. "If that gold is goin' north, it has to follow the river."

"Which leaves us a problem, *amigo*." Brava stroked his mustache. "Has our wagon gone north? Or is someone riding to Blanco to take the last one?"

"Jesus!" Vansittart spat. "I don't know. The goddam ground's too hard to read tracks. Maybe we was wrong coming north. Maybe the gold got took southwards."

"No." Brava shook his head. "That crazy *gringo* was on the north side of the canyon. If the wagon had gone south, he'd have been that side. It must be going back to Green Springs."

"So?" Vansittart shrugged. "What do we do? Split up? One take the high road and one take the low?"

"We stay together," said Brava. "I have thought this out, and what I decided was that we don't trust each other. If we split up, then we both will try to take all the gold. If we stay together, we can maybe find both wagons and stay friends. Rich friends."

"So which trail do we take fer Chrissakes?" asked the American. "Or we gonna argue about that?"

"No." Brava grinned, the movement lifting the waxed points of his mustache up towards his bland eyes. "We go across the high patch. I know this country, so I know that a wagon must take the lower trail. From the Las Cruces canyon to Green Springs it is maybe a week's ride. A man on horseback can cut right down on that time. If he follows the high trail and rides hard, then he can get there inside four days. That's why we shall both take the high road, my friend."

"Fine," said Vansittart. 'Let's go."

Hawk reached the place where the trails split and wondered over the same problems. He was tired after spending two nights awake, and angry with himself and Ben Galant for letting a carefully-set plan fall apart.

He decided to follow the obvious path

of the wagon: the only one it could take. Down towards the river.

He rode as hard as he dared for the sandy stretch of trail, denying himself sleep, but resting the black horse. He was —he guessed—two hours behind the outlaws, and he wanted to catch up on that period.

He was almost there when they killed Billy Garrett.

Billy was long clear of the meadow and pushing his mules fast after the lazy rest. He thought to be in Green Springs inside of two days, without any sign of pursuit. It was funny that neither Ben nor Hawk had caught up with him, but he decided that was because they had gone off after the outlaws. Maybe trailing them down into Mexico.

If that was the case, then he would be the hero of the day. He'd be the one who brought the gold home. One wagonload, at least. On his own.

Like a hero.

Ben Parmalee would recognize him as a solid, reliable man.

As a real gunfighter.

As good as Jared Hawk.

With a bonus coming, and maybe even more money after that.

And then the guns took all his hopes away and spread them in bloody fragments of pain-filled nightmare over the sun-kissed grass.

Brava and Vansittart had come out from the high trail a full day's ride ahead of Billy Garrett. It had taken them a long time of hard riding. Cutting through draws and climbing steep banks. Not eating. Just thinking about the gold and riding hard enough to get in front of the wagon.

Far enough in front that they could take up positions either side of the trail while they waited for Billy to appear.

It was a stretch of bare rock, flanked on the west side by a sheer drop that fell down a thousand feet or more to the gravel bottom of the river. On the east side there were cliffs that lifted up just as high.

Towering walls of wind-washed stone, bleak and bare and empty. The trail led past a curve in that implacable frontage.

It led past the curve into a stretch where the trail got worse, narrowing down over a stone bridge that spanned a thin gulley flanked on both sides by cutaways of secondary water.

Luis Brava was inside one cutaway, on the landward flank of the mountains; Cole Vansittart in the other, on the river side.

They shot Billy Garrett together.

Both men were using Winchesters, firing from close range, their positions ensuring that the youngster handling the gold-laden wagon was caught in a cross-fire. Their only problem was the danger of panicking the mules, or maybe wounding an animal, so that the team went over the cliff and spilled the gold into the river. For that reason they had agreed a simple plan: both men would open fire on the driver, aiming for head shots so as to kill him fast without allowing him time to lift the mules to a gallop or turn the wagon. Then Brava, who was slightly closer to the trail, would grab the reins while Vansittart came up from the west side to drive the team back against the safety of the inner cliff.

The American tilted his black stetson down over his eyes, shading out the sun as he watched the wagon getting closer. He wiped his hands against the legs of his black pants and squinted through the brilliance to where Luis crouched behind a boulder. For a moment he thought about shooting the Mexican; killing him and taking all the gold for himself. After all, it had been his contact in Green Springs who put them on to this particular deal, and so far Brava hadn't done much to help it along, except bluster a lot and foul up. The whole damn' thing had been going wrong from the time they stashed the three wagons, and Vansittart had an ugly feeling that more trouble was coming. He couldn't say exactly why, but it was funny that Charley Braco and Wade Strother hadn't showed up in Las Cruces. And the fact that someone had known where the second wagon was hidden indicated that they were dead: there was no other way anyone could know about the old Indian burial canyon. Unless Brava had told them.

But if that was the case, then why was Brava so intent on chasing the other two? Greed? Or did he really not know what was happening?

Vansittart wiped sweat from his face and decided to leave Luis alive. After all, two wagons loaded with gold would take some handling, and the Mexican had contacts south of the border that could prove very useful when it came to disposing of the loot.

Across the narrowing of the trail, Luis Brava was thinking along much the same lines. He decided against trying to kill the *gringo* for two reasons. The first was a parallel of Vansittart's thought: two wagons needed two men; the second was the doubt that he might not be successful: Cole was very fast and very tricky.

He stroked his mustache, thinking that maybe when they got all the gold over the border he would try something. After all, even Vansittart had to sleep sometime.

He folded the forward edge of his sombrero back against the crown and thumbed the hammer of his carbine to full cock. The wagon was getting steadily closer.

Billy Garrett hummed softly, scanning the ground ahead. So far there had been no sign of pursuit, and now that he was drawing closer to Green Springs he was beginning to feel even more confident. The fact that neither Ben nor Hawk had caught up with him was a little worrying, but that slight doubt was overcome by the absence of hostile pursuit. It could always be that Hawk had gone further south after the thieves and Ben had taken the high trail to get ahead of him.

Yeah, he decided, that must be it. Hawk had said one man would come after the wagon, no matter what, so Ben was probably waiting up ahead, chewing tobacco and grumbling about the time it was taking the wagon to reach him.

And then Billy had a second thought: if Ben could take the high trail and get in front, then so could anyone else. Instantly, his humming stopped and his hooded eyes snapped wide open. There were plenty of places along the road that outlaws could mount an ambush. The best locations—the ones Billy would choose, had he gone that road—were on the meadows, where the wagon had to slow to negotiate the flanking trees or the downfalls of spilled stone. He stared hard at the terrain in front of him: it wasn't a good place. The trail was narrow, banked on one side by high cliffs, on the other by a sheer drop. It left little room for manoeuvre, so that an ambusher might get run down by the mules or shoved over the edge. It made no sense to mount an attack there, where a single wrong move might tip a man down a sheer rockface, or plaster him against a hard, stone wall. No sense at all. Billy relaxed, chuckling at his own doubts.

Which was exactly why Luis Brava and Cole Vansittart had chosen that position.

The Mexican fired first. He waited until the wagon was level with his position, then stepped clear of the boulder and triggered a shot at Billy's head. The movement caught Billy's eye, so that he turned in the seat, lifting up to clutch at the Colt holstered on his right hip.

His movement was fractional, but it raised him high enough and fast enough that the .44-40 slug missed its target: his right temple. Instead, due to the upwards twisting movement of his body, it hit his throat, entering just beneath his jaw into the web of flesh covering the neck. It cut through the fragile tissue and ploughed a bloody mark over his Adam's apple. A thick swathe of blood flushed from his neck, covering his chest with crimson.

Instinct planted him sideways across the seat of the Studebaker and lifted his right hand up from the holster with the Colt bucking flame at the rocks.

As he fell, Cole Vansittart fired once into his back. The bullet hit as Billy was falling. It went in under his left shoulder, tearing through the trapezoid muscle to deflect off the shoulder-blade in a thin spray of blood that splattered against Billy's face.

His left arm went numb. There was no pain, only a total cessation of feeling, and as though in a dream he saw his left hand clasp the reins and drag them back, turning the mules to the left. At the same time he went on firing, blasting five bullets against the rockface. Towards the smoke and flame of the Mexican's carbine.

Brava fired again, putting a slug into the youngster's right shoulder. It went in through the knob of muscle covering the apex of the joint. Tore out in a fountain of scarlet that covered the right side of Billy's face with smearing redness before lodging in the underside of his jaw, close against the joint of mouth and neck.

Billy tried hard to scream; but the shots had damaged his vocal cords so that all that came out was a single hoarse cry.

Brava came running out from the cover of the boulders, and Vansittart came up waving at the frightened mules.

The force of the bullets, and his own protective action, had thrown Billy Garrett leftways across the wagon. Throughout the brief moments of firing he had kept the reins over to the west side of the trail: to where the cliff went down towards the distant glitter of the Rio Grande.

Now the left-hand lead mule began to buck as the controlling leathers hauled its mouth over towards the gap. Its eyes rolled, reddened by fear and gunsmoke, and when Luis Brava ran towards it, it swung its hooves round and tried to kick him. Which meant that its companion in harness—equally frightened—took the force of the blows and shifted away, bucking in turn.

A hoof struck Brava, landing hard against his spreading belly as he tried to fasten a hand on the reins. He groaned and doubled over, stumbling clear of the team.

Vansittart came up from his side of the trail and saw the mules plunging in wild confusion. He levered his Winchester and shot the left-side lead animal through the skull. It was a neat, tidy shot, fired from the hip. It went in between the black-haired space separating the eye from the ear, crashing the bone inwards to rip through the membranes of the brain.

It killed the mule instantly, plunging out through the right ear to leave a sticky swelter of blood and brain matter against the farther cliff.

The mule jerked sideways, then reflex action sprang its legs into rigid lines that lifted it in a high, sideways buck. It came a good four feet off the ground, and when it landed, it was two feet clear of the trail's edge.

Its body landed loose over the rim of the cliff, the tugging reins hauling Billy Garrett clear of the wagon's seat, yanking him from the Studebaker behind the dead mule.

He hit the rim and got dragged over as the right-hand animal squealed a shrill protest and followed its companion down over the cliff into the space below.

The reins snatched loose from Billy's hand as he struck a bush growing out from the cliff. They rasped over his skin, tearing solid chunks of flesh loose, but his body stayed hooked over the shrubbery, blood pulsing from his neck and face, his arms useless.

There was a moment of relative quiet as the remaining mules fought the drag on the harness and fought to stay clear of the cliff. They snorted and stamped their hooves against the hardness of the rock, which gave them little purchase, so that the weight of the two already fallen over the edge dragged them slowly closer.

"Jesus!" Vansittart put his shoulder hard against the left-side forward wheel. "Get the goddam brake."

Luis Brava clutched his bruised belly and spat vomit from his mouth, running over to the wagon as a third mule lost its footing on the edge and began to scream in panic.

He got up on to the wagon and snatched the brake back.

But it was too late.

The third mule was already screaming as the first two hauled it over the rimrock, their combined weight dragging it sideways over the edge. Its teamed companion joined it, then the last pair. And the left-side front wheel of the wagon spun in empty circles over nothing but a thousand feet of drop.

Vansittart jumped away, ducking under the spinning circle of the wheel. Brava jumped to the far side of the trail. And the wagon tilted over, the base catching for an instant on the rimrock, lifting the inside wheel up in wild circles that spun light off the spokes and seemed to counterpoint the screeching of the base against the stone as the whole thing slid sideways There was a moment of silence when the first rear wheel hauled clear of the cliff and the other spun quietly, the spokes darting shards of light back against the stone of the trail's wall.

Then the metal rim of the left-side wheel grated noisily against the hard edge of the cliff, and the bed of the Studebaker tilted sideways, raining a black cloud of tarpaulin and a finer fragmentation of shimmering ingots down towards the waiting waters of the river. And the whole thing went over.

The tarpaulin caught the wind blowing along the river bed, lifting up and fluttering like some black messenger of death above the plummeting bodies of the mules and Billy Garrett's horse. The animals struck the rocks and bounced away, shattering so that they left enormous smears of blood and opened organs down the sides of the drop. Between them, like a rain of gold, the ingots danced over bare rock and bloody corpses, splashing into the river after leaving streaks of soft promise through the blood and the entrails.

Down below, far below, the gold raised splashes from the water.

And Cole Vansittart looked at Luis Brava and said, "We lost two. Let's try to keep the last one."

"*Si*," said Brava. "There is something going badly wrong here. I think we cut out our losses and take what we got left."

"Yeah," said the American. "Trouble is, we ain't got much now. We're getting cut down all the way."

"Don't get deflated," said Brava. "We can always thatch something together. Like the good saint Margaret says, it's how you do it, not the way."

11

HAWK came up off the low trail a day or more after Billy Garrett was spread over the bush. By then he was feeling mad at Ben Galant for jumping the outlaws in his own time and failing to tell him about the faster route north.

He got even more angry when he saw the buzzards curling over Billy's body and reined in where the fresh chippings of stone decorated the rockface.

The pockmarks of the bullets could have been old—it was hard to tell from that kind of stone—but the spiral of dark-pinioned birds was clear evidence of fresh meat.

He reined in and peered over the rim.

The first thing he saw was a smear of black over the rocks at the foot of the cliff. Closer observation defined the smears as the bodies of mules and a horse. It was hard to pick out the shapes because they were spread like jam, and carrion crows were clustered in squadrons of black alongside the buzzards and vultures over the shattered shapes. The horse was spread, sway-backed where its spine had broken over a rock, in an obscene vee-shape that had burst the belly and left it wide for the birds. Most of the mules had fallen into the river and got carried south, but two were still draggled over the shale with birds plucking the entrails from their opened stomachs.

And across a stubby spread of branches that stuck out from the bare rock like angry fingers clutching at the sky there was Billy Garrett.

He was draped loose and bloody over the limbs of the bush. Hung like a piece of meat in a butcher's shop, awaiting the decision that would render him down into single pieces of meat.

The crows perching on his shoulders and waist seemed to be waiting for the same decision. The only reason they held off their pecking was the dull moaning of the boy.

Hawk edged over to look at him.

Saw an impossible problem: Billy was hung like a slab of meat over a scrubby bush. His face was covered with blood, more coming from the holes in his back and the raw wound on his left wrist. He was still breathing, but each movement of his body pumped fresh spurts of blood clear from his back and face. There was a thin column of ants walking vertically down the rockface and then out along the tree, clambering over the body and returning up the same route to their holes.

Hawk cursed the delay and lifted his rope clear of the saddle. Then he fastened one end around a stanchion of rock and looped a secondary knot over his saddle-horn. The lariat held sufficient length that he was able to fashion a fresh loop and drop enough past Billy's body that he had ten feet clear.

He began to climb down the cliff, good right hand fastened tight about the cord, the numbed fingers of his gloved left hand feeding the rope up and back from under his buttocks, the absence of friction allowing him to hold it close against the downswing.

He reached Billy and knotted the rope into a firm hold.

Eased the noose upwards and got it looped around the youngster's waist.

Billy groaned as the rope drew tight, lifting his head to fasten a pain-dulled stare on Hawk's dangling body. The crows took off in raucous flight, and the combination of movements shifted the youngster's body round so that it tilted clear of the bush. Hawk grunted a curse and fastened both hands tight around the rope, bracing his feet against the rock.

There was a shock that threatened to jerk his grip loose, and the taut rope twanged like a massive guitar string. The gunfighter felt the muscles across his back and through his arms knot hard as they fought to control the shock, and then his feet were sprung loose from the cliff by the pendulum swing of the deadweight below. For long moments he swung across the face of the stone, hands and elbows and knees grating against the rock. He closed his eyes, fighting the dizziness that threatened to numb his senses and confuse him enough that he let go and fell down to join Parmalee's gold on the rocks of the river bed.

Then the black horse squealed a shrill protest and began to struggle back against the drag of the rope. Hawk was lifted upwards. Felt his face grate against stone. And then scrabbled his legs up until he had both feet once more braced against the cliff. Slowly, painfully, he began to walk up the vertical face. His body shrieked painful warnings along the nerves of his arms and legs, and sweat burst from his face, blurring his vision so that he climbed in a dull haze that was lit only by the redness of the effort.

He got to the rim and hauled himself over, stretching, mouth wide open as he sucked in great lungfuls of air and waited for the pain to recede, across the trail.

When he felt confident of staying upright, he climbed to his feet and looked down. Billy Garret was hanging quiet against the cliff, head lower than his feet so that a steady dripping of blood fell from his face and shoulders.

Hawk went over to the horse and gentled it down. Climbed into the saddle and urged the animal forwards. It took a long time, because he was wary of fraying the rope against the angle of the rim, but he got Billy up on solid ground and loosed the rope from the boy's waist.

Billy's face, under its overlay of dried blood, was pale. Patches of skin had been rubbed away by the ascent, and where the bullets had struck him, his flesh was swollen with the ugly signs of poison. Both arms were slack appendages, the right broken at the shoulder so that a curious knob of protruding bone jutted up in a hump beside his neck.

Hawk folded a blanket under his head and dribbled water between his lips.

"I guess I lost it," mumbled Billy. "Sorry."

"Not your fault," said Hawk. "It was Ben fouled things."

"Where is he?" Billy asked. "What happened?"

"Dead," Hawk answered. "He tried to play too smart. Tried to jump them. That's how they caught up with you."

"Guess he never liked takin' orders from no one except Ben Parmalee." Billy's voice got fainter. "I think I'm dyin'. I bust some ribs when I fell down an' I think yore rope put them into my lungs."

As though to confirm his diagnosis, he coughed up a stream of bright blood.

"I'm sorry," Hawk said. "I couldn't leave you there."

"No." The slack folding of the youngster's mouth was a parody of a smile. "I'd have done the same."

"Who was it?" Hawk asked. "How many?"

"Two. Like you reckoned." Billy's voice got even more lost, so that Hawk had to bend close to the bloody face to hear the words. "A Mex an' a Southerner. The Mex got hurt when a mule kicked him."

"They say anything?" Hawk put the canteen back against Billy's lips. "Like where they was going?"

"Sounded like Blanco Canyon," said the kid. "Sounded like they was due to meet someone there. I couldn't hear too well."

"No," said Hawk. "You wouldn't."

"Don't leave me out here," said Billy. "I don't want to die out here."

"I won't," Hawk said. "I'll stay with you."

Billy said, "Thanks," and closed his eyes. Blood came out from his nostrils and he doubled up as he began to choke. He opened his mouth to spit great gobbets of blood over his chest as Hawk held him and tried to calm him. And then his teeth grated together and his legs thrust rigid, and from deep down in his throat came a rattling sound that ended in a whisper. His eyes opened once, then closed again. Forever. His body went slack.

Hawk stood up.

He looped his rope into a neat coil and slung it back on his saddle. Then he fed the black horse a measure of oats and turned to Billy's corpse. He stared at the body for a while, thinking about all the times the same thing might have happened to him, and folded the hands over the chest.

Then he put his foot against Billy's right side and rolled the corpse over the edge of the cliff.

It went down in a curve that took it clear of the rockface for most of the distance. When it hit, the counterthrust of stone and plummeting flesh hurled it outwards in a tangle of flailing limbs over the water. There was a splash that lifted the vultures and crows in screaming confusion from the rotting corpses of the animals, and it began to drift away, twisting over as the current took it.

Hawk watched until it was gone out of sight.

It was almost like watching a fragment of his own life drift away.

"Sorry, kid," he murmured, "but I don't have time to dig holes. Not with a spade."

12

HAWK rode in the direction of Green Springs through the brilliant twilight of a late summer day. The air was warm, and once he came clear of the rocky terrain, the evening got loud with birdsong. Beyond the section of stony ground, the trail led into a series of folding meadows and long, wide streamers of trees that came down off the peaks in wide folds that tumbled in a kaleidoscope of colours to the banks of the river.

Conifers stood tall and green and stately over the upper levels of the land; below them, shading down into the canyons, there were cottonwoods and aspens and cedars, green and gold and silver contrasting with the sombre hues of the oaks that stood like knurled guardians over darker patches of grass. The ground itself was a patchwork of colours: the hard blue of the bedrock giving way to the yellow of sandstone, the striations combining to produce a profusion of shades that were cut through by the green of the meadows. And in the grassy places there were poppies and sunflowers and clumps of a blue growth that he didn't recognize.

No more than he saw them as he pushed the black horse along the trail leading back to town.

Back to town and Blanco Canyon.

There was a sour feeling settled deep in his gut: a combination of anger and hate and disgust. He wanted to kill Luis Brava and Cole Vansittart for what they had done to him. That was a personal debt: an owing of balances that might only be worked out on the personal scales of life. He had also undertaken to do a job for Ben Parmalee, and that job had been fouled up by Ben Galant. Hawk blamed himself for that: he should have done it alone. The way he liked to work. Then Billy Garrett had died. Mostly because Galant had failed to tell Hawk where the trails split and tried his own thing, but even so—Hawk told himself—he should have made certain of his men before accepting them as companions. And Billy did remind him of himself: young and cocky. Trusting the more experienced hands to back him up, without the knowledge of people that might have told him there's no way to trust anyone except yourself.

Like Valentinas . . .

In Sonora . . .

Mexico . . .

A hot afternoon in July . . .

Flies buzzing over the tequila pots, and the heat lifting dust-devils from the plaza . . .

Hawk had sipped the fierce liquor and waited for the Mexican to show up, staring out through the bead curtain fronting the cantina, confident that Juliano would shown soon and tell him which of the three they were hunting were in the cantina. Which were out on the plaza.

Juliano Valentinas was ten years older than Jared Hawk, and the young American trusted him because the Mexican bounty hunter had already given him fifty dollars American to be taken out of their shared reward for the three Guyamos brothers.

Juliano had gone out to ask some questions: to find out where the brothers were hiding. It had made sense to leave Jared in the cantina, because then he didn't speak Spanish too well and Juliano came from a village close to Sonora.

Somewhere along the line of communications Juliano had made a deal with the Guyamos brothers.

He walked into the cantina with a wide smile on his face and Raul and Pedro coming in behind him. Rafael had come in through the back door and put a .45 calibre slug through the lantern landing three inches over Jared's head.

The mistake in aim had proved the death of the Mexican and his brothers.

Jared had spilled out of his chair and squeezed a single shot into Rafael's belly. While the Mexican outlaw was still going down with his mouth barely opened wide enough to release the scream, Jared was turning his gun on the others.

He had noticed that Juliano was trying to climb over the bar, not backing his partner.

Jared shot Raul and Pedro, and when Juliano showed his face again, he had shot him. Just once. Neatly, through the bridge of the nose, destroying the face so that Juliano Valentinas slammed back against the shelves with his brains bleeding out over the dusty bottles.

, When Hawk checked his body, he found one hundred dollars in new notes tucked inside the fancy vest. The notes the Guyamos brothers had given Juliano to betray his partner.

And since then, Hawk had trusted no one . . .

No one at all . . .

He rode on, trying the strength of the black stallion as he pushed the pace towards the final confrontation.

It had to happen in either Blanco Canyon or Green Springs. The informer came from the town and—presumably— had a date to meet Brava and Vansittart to divide up his share of the gold. It seemed unlikely that either of the outlaws would risk going into town—at least, not unless they were confident of finding a safe welcome and somewhere to hide. Which narrowed down the possible helpers to the people who knew about Parmalee's gold shipments.

Hawk decided to speak with the mine owner.

He came out from the open some time after sunset. Over to the west the big red disc was throwing patterns of light across the sky that were getting eaten by the darkness spreading from the east. A few stars were already visible, and low in the sky there was the face of a full moon, shining a waxy yellow like a melting candle. Or a corpse.

Hawk reined in, studying the ground separating him from the mine.

Hoping that Parmalee was there, and not in Green Springs.

He trailed along the rimrock, taking the patch Ben Galant had showed him when they rode out, and following it down to a position above and eastwards of the cabin. He dismounted there and tethered the black horse inside a ring of trees far enough back from the split that it would not be seen. Then he took his Winchester and began the long walk down.

It was full night before he reached the cabin. The moon was drifting lazily over the sky, its yellow face smeared with the fumes from the smelting sheds that rose up in palpable waftings to spread a kind of fog across the calm clarity of the night. There were lights from the windows of the cabin and the sound of voices.

Hawk waited, crouched down against a tall rock that covered him with shadow and afforded a degree of protection from the chilly wind that had gotten up out of the east.

After a while the door of the cabin opened to spread a wide beam of light over the trail leading down to the bowl of the valley. Three men came out. One was fat and easily recognizable as Sheriff Buford Stoker. The second was shorter and skinnier, dressed in a black robe, like a priest, the impression confirmed by the round-crowned hat he had settled on his head. The third was tall and thin, wearing a grey suit, like a banker or a lawyer. Hawk watched Parmalee bid farewell, holding the door open so that their path down was lit until they reached the area where the mine workings afforded them clear illumination. The priest and the man in the grey suit climbed on to the seat of a buckboard. Stoker mounted a horse. And all three headed down the mountain in the direction of Green Springs.

Hawk moved down the side of the hill behind them, working silently towards the cabin.

He reached the front and tapped on the door.

When it opened, he shoved the muzzle of the Winchester up against Parmalee's stomach and stepped inside.

He heeled the door shut and said, "Who's with you?"

"No one." Parmalee stepped back from the rifle. "What happened?"

"Trouble," said Hawk, lowering the hammer of the Winchester. "You got a drink?"

Parmalee nodded, filling a glass with whisky. Hawk took it and sat down. Parmalee took a seat facing him.

"You want to tell me?"

"We found the wagon," said Hawk. "Right where I said it would be. Even got it out."

"Where is it now?" interrupted the old man. "You bring it back?"

"No." Hawk shook his head. "It was all lined up, but then Ben Galant got too clever. He jumped them before we was ready an' got himself killed. That gave them the chance to get ahead an' wait up for Billy."

"Yeah?" Parmalee reached out to fill the glasses again. "What about Billy?"

"They killed him," said Hawk flatly "Shot him up an' spilled the wagon over a cliff. The gold's on the bottom of the Rio Grande."

"Goddam it!" grunted Parmalee. "You lost it. How about the third?"

"Still in Blanco Canyon, I guess." Hawk emptied his glass and yawned. "They might try takin' it out, but I got a feeling they'll wait for the man set them on to the raid."

"Why?" Parmalee asked. "Why should they?"

"I'm not sure," Hawk replied, "it's mostly a feeling, nothing more. They left one wagon there when they could've taken it south. But Braco said they was planning to split with the informer, so they must rate him pretty high. Pretty useful."

He sipped his whisky and stared at the fire.

"Who'd know about your gold, Parmalee? Who could give Vansittart that information?"

The mine owner shrugged. "A lotta people. No one. It depends."

"On what?" Hawk asked. "Tell me. All of it."

"Anyone around the mine could know when we got a load to ship out," said Parmalee, "just by watchin' the sheds and the loading bays. We fine it down here then shift it into town ready for shippin' out. Mostly it's small loads, guarded by riders. I keep enough men around to scare off most owlhooters."

"But this time Brava knew there was a big load," said Hawk. "Who'd be able to tell him that?"

"I could," said Parmalee. "Dale Evans, in the bank. Stoker. My foreman, Vern Thomas. No one else."

"No one?" asked Hawk. "No one at all?"

"Not for sure," said Parmalee. "The people up here would know we shifted a lotta gold, but they wouldn't know when it was going out."

"The guards would know," said Hawk. "Men like Ben Galant. Billy Garrett."

"Wouldn't be worth their while." Parmalee shook his head. "I pay them too well, an' they know what I'd do to find them if they did doublecross me. They know they got steady work with me. Well-paid. Not be worth it to lose all that."

"Someone set it up," said Hawk. "If it

wasn't a guard, then how about Stoker? Or the banker?"

"I just fed Buford a gutful o' liquor," said Parmalee. "I wanted to sweeten him up because he knows it was me bust you outta jail. He ain't sayin' as much, but he still knows. He's a relatively honest man —wants to hold on to his badge an' still feel independent. Like Dale Evans. Christ! They both know it's my money keepin' them in office."

"They could get greedy," suggested Hawk. "Want a bit more. And like you say, they'd know when the gold was going through."

"It don't make sense," said Parmalee. "If Stoker wanted to take it, then all he'd need do was ride out with the wagons an' fix an ambush along the trail. When it happened, he took a posse out all the way to the border. If he'd really wanted to lift that gold, he needn't have done more than let it happen and take his share. An' he wouldn't be here now, he'd be in Mexico."

He shook his head and poured more whisky.

"Same applies to Dale Evans. He's about as upright a little toad as you can imagine. He knows that the first bit of scandal attaches is gonna lose him promotion. He also knows he does real good outta me. An' if he wanted to steal gold, he'd do it on paper. Pare off a little each month an' quit when he had enough stashed someplace."

Hawk emptied his glass and set it aside, thinking hard. Somewhere down the line there had to be a link. The girl, Johanna, was a connection, but he didn't know how to fix her in.

"What about Johanna?" he asked.

"A whore." Parmalee shrugged. "She came into town a year an' a half back. I remember the day."

He chuckled, shaking his head from side to side, fluttering the thick folds of his silvery hair.

"Was real funny, her an' Father Durant arriving at the same time. We'd never had a regular priest nor a regular whore. The girls we got mostly moved on after a while. Headed for better pastures, I guess. An' we never got a permanent preacher until we built a regular church. Then Johanna an' the Father come in together. Same goddam stage, believe it or not! The one climbed down all dark and serious, asking where his chapel was located and how big was the congregation, while the other come out blonde an' excitin', asking was there a room in the saloon she could take over."

Hawk shrugged, dismissing the old man's reminiscences.

"She ever tie in to anyone in particular?" he asked. "Someone who might send her to me to find out what I was doing for you?"

"No one." Parmalee went on chuckling as he shook his head. "She just took herself a room in the St. Lawrence an' smiled at everyone. Jesus! I recall how Liz got jealous when she saw Sid smilin' at Johanna. Gettin' visions, I guess."

"So there's no one you know would put

her up to that?" said Hawk. "Not to sleeping with me and pulling a gun?"

"No one at all," said Parmalee. "She was a whore, but everyone liked her. Even Father Durant. Christ! I never seen a man so upset as him, when we buried her."

Something sparkled inside Hawk's mind. It was like the fragments of two half-forgotten dreams coming together in the memory to make up part of a whole. Not complete, but building in the direction of a total picture, with just a few pieces left to find and slot into place.

"You don't know her last name?" he asked.

"No," Parmalee shrugged, still smiling. "She was just Johanna."

"And she came in on the same stage as Father Durant?"

"Yeah. Like I told you: the black an' the red together."

"What's Durant's full name?" Hawk asked. "You know that?"

Parmalee spread his hands in a gesture of bewilderment. "Who knows a priest's proper name? He's Father Durant. That's all. Why?"

"He's Catholic?"

Hawk pushed his glass aside, ignoring Parmalee's offer, sitting forwards in his chair with his weariness forgotten.

"Sure. I guess." Parmalee shrugged. "I gotta confess I ain't overly taken with all that stuff. But yeah, I guess he's Catholic."

"So if you were sending out a shipment of gold," said Hawk slowly, "with guards on it—men liable to kill others, or get killed themselves—if they were Catholics, they'd go to confession, wouldn't they?"

"I guess so," said Parmalee. "What you getting at?"

"You said there was only the few men knew your gold was going out," said Hawk. "Now there's another."

"Durant?" Parmalee laughed. "That skirted mother wouldn't dare cross a spavined cow, let alone me."

"Perhaps," said Hawk, "but I think I'll confess some sins tomorrow. And maybe collect a few. How does lying to a priest count?"

"I don't know," said Parmalee. "I'm a Protestant."

"So don't confess," said Hawk. "Just leave me to protest."

13

"FORGIVE me, Father, for I have sinned."

"What is the nature of your sin?" Durant's voice was muffled by the thick curtain dividing the confessional box.

"*Sins*," Hawk corrected. "In the plural. Leastways, I guess you'd call them sins."

"You are not a Catholic, are you?" The priest sounded doubtful. "Why have you come to me?"

"Reckoned you wouldn't bother too much which persuasion I follow." Hawk chose his words carefully. "I thought you people were around to help everyone."

"True," Durant still sounded wary, "but it is unusual for a man not of our faith to seek the solace of confession."

"There's a first time for everything." Hawk stared into the darkness of the cupboard-like booth, willing the priest to take the bait. If the wild idea that had come to him in Parmalee's cabin was right, then the next few minutes could precipitate the confrontation he sought. "Ain't that so?"

There was a pause, and he could hear Durant's breathing: short and sharp, like a man wrestling with some inner problem. The church was quiet at this hour of the morning, the early service concluded and the few worshippers gone back to their homes or businesses. Hawk had seen him only once before, and that fleetingly, in the early hours of a misty morning. He had not recognized the gunfighter, ushering him into the divided booth with only the slightest flicker of interest. It was a long time since Hawk had been inside a church, and his opening statement was based on some half-forgotten memory, as was his plan.

The strategy depended on him revealing himself as the man Parmalee had hired to track down the thieves. On revealing just about everything that had happened, including the return of Brava and Vansittart to Blanco Canyon. At that point it was possible that Durant would start yelling for the sheriff, but Hawk recalled a man he had known once—a devout Catholic —telling him that everything said in the confessional was held in confidence, that the priest was under a holy vow to keep secret the revelations granted him. Hawk couldn't be sure that rule applied to non-Catholics. Couldn't even be certain Durant would agree to hear him out.

In that case, he had decided, he would force the skinny padre to listen—at gunpoint if necessary. And if Durant hollered for the law, then Hawk could be up and gone before Stoker had a chance to start shooting.

Durant sighed and said, "Very well, I will listen to your confession. But I cannot grant you absolution."

Hawk wasn't sure what that meant, but it sounded like things were going the way he wanted.

"I shot some people," he said. "That's mostly what I get paid to do."

There was a sudden intake of breath

from the other side of the curtain, but when Durant spoke his voice was controlled.

"How many?" he asked. "Are you an officer of the law?"

"I never bothered to count." Hawk shrugged in the darkness, right hand brushing the polished leather of his holster, wondering if he was meant to feel guilty. "An' I'm not a lawman."

"Two men? Five?" Durant's fingers clicked nervously over the beads of his rosary. "More?"

"More."

The priest murmured a brief prayer, then: "Are you a bounty hunter?"

"I've hunted bounty," Hawk confirmed. "Fought in range wars. Shot folks as was tryin' to kill me."

"And now you feel remorse?" Durant's voice was carefully modulated, encouraging a positive response. "That is why you came here? To seek comfort in the arms of the Church?"

"Something like that," said Hawk.

"The last person I killed was a woman. A whore called Johanna."

"My God!" Durant's cry was mid-way between a gasp of pure shock and a prayer. "You're Parmalee's hired man! The one who broke jail."

"Yeah," said Hawk; slowly. "You gonna turn me in?"

His hand settled around the butt of the Colt, thumb resting lightly on the hammer. From the other side of the curtain he could hear the clicking of the beads, the priest's nervous breathing. For a long time Durant said nothing.

Then, slowly: "No. You have sinned horribly, and I am not sure you will ever find absolution, but I cannot betray your trust. You came to me, a sinner steeped deep in guilt, but you sought to unburden your sins. I cannot betray that faith."

In the darkness, Hawk smiled; cold and mean, like a waiting wolf. And like a wolf, he pushed his prey a little farther down the line that would lead to the waiting jaws.

"She took a shot at me," he said into

the silence. "The outlaws Parmalee hired me to find sent her, I guess. Leastways, she was tryin' to find out how much I knew when she pulled the gun."

"And you killed her." Durant's voice was dull.

"Wasn't much else I could do." In a way it was true: Hawk was a creature of instinct, and shooting Johanna had been a purely instinctive reaction to the fact of her drawing a gun. You pulled a gun on a man—or a woman—and you better be ready to use it, to take the chance of them firing back. "No more'n with the two I found down in Calaveros."

"Calaveros?" asked Durant. "That was after you escaped the jail?"

"Trailed them there," said Hawk. "They came at me, so I killed them. I got Parmalee's gold back an' a lead on the other two."

"All of it?" Durant's voice was different now. It was hard to tell if the change in tone expressed interest, or firmly-imposed control, designed to conceal the revulsion he felt. "What happened to the others?"

"Just two wagons," said Hawk. "Luis Brava an' Cole Vansittart got away."

"I understood three were taken." Durant coughed. Just once. "That's what mister Parmalee told me."

"Yeah." Hawk felt tense as the final piece of bait got thrown down. "Makes me feel bad—about lettin' Parmalee down, I mean. Looks like they hid the third wagon somewhere near here. I lost them on the trail. They was headin' back this way, though."

Again, Durant was quiet. Hawk waited for him to speak.

"I cannot grant you absolution," said the priest at last, "only advice. I urge you to give up this way of life. Put down your guns. Cast them in the river. Let them wash on out to sea. Continue to use them, and that big dark cloud will come down when you cannot use them any more. You will find yourself knocking on Heaven's door with only blood on the tracks behind you. Lest the fire in the wind take you, go away from here! Forget these outlaws. Forget killing! Wash the blood from your hands and try to live amongst the decent people. Perhaps in time you may find salvation."

"I'll quit Green Springs," said Hawk. "But what about the sheriff? You won't tell Stoker?"

"No." The priest's voice was firm now, empty of doubt. "I shall pray for you, but I will not tell the sheriff."

"Thanks," said Hawk. "You helped me more than you know."

"God go with you," intoned Durant. "I will pray for you."

"Yeah."

Hawk drew the curtain back from the upper part of the doorway. Opened the half door at the bottom. His boots thudded loud on the scrubbed planking of the floor, and for no reason he could define, he kept his hat in his hand until he reached the porch. When he turned, just outside the main doors, Father Durant was on his knees before the low altar, hands clasped together—tight—and head bowed against his chest.

Hawk went round the church and

mounted the black horse. Then he rode hard and fast for Parmalee's cabin.

The guards on the gate recognized him and let him through. The mine workings were in full production and few people bothered to watch him as he climbed up to the cabin. The day was bright now, though above the bowl containing the mine there was a drifting fug of oily smoke and the air was reeking with the stink of the smelting sheds; of heated oil and burning timber, sweat, horse dung, and the acrid stench of hot metal.

He went into the cabin and found it empty, so he helped himself to coffee. A clock on the wall showed five minutes after ten. He settled into a chair facing the door and waited.

After a while, during which time the hands of the clock moved with agonizing slowness round to ten minutes before eleven, Parmalee showed up.

His piercing blue eyes were alight with interest, and he went straight to the liquor cabinet, filling two glasses with whisky.

"Well? What happened?"

Hawk shrugged, accepting the drink.

"I told him. He told me to quit town an' get some quiet work. You?"

"Like we agreed." Parmalee paced around the floor, too excited to sit down or stay still. "I gave Evans the story an' let it out to Sid in the St. Lawrence. That guarantees it gets spread all over town by noon."

"You didn't name Blanco Canyon?" asked Hawk; warily.

"No!" Parmalee shook his head. "Just told 'em my own men got two wagons back an' the outlaws was comin' north again to pick up the third. Durant won't say anythin' different, will he?"

"He said he wouldn't say anything at all." Hawk shook his head. "So now everyone likely to have tipped off the Brava gang knows there's only one wagon left, an' just Luis an' Vansittart coming back to get it. That should stir something up. Your people all accounted for?"

"Sure." Parmalee nodded. "I got everyone tied up with work for the next week. The guards are operating in three-somes, an' I got watches mounted on the diggers. There's no way anyone who works for me can slip outta town."

"Fine," said Hawk. "That makes it simple. I'll ride up to the canyon an' wait. I doubt the informer will take long gettin' there, not when he thinks he could lose his share."

"Suppose he don't?" asked Parmalee. "What then?"

"Brava an' Vansittart will show up," said Hawk. "I'll kill them. I reckon the third man'll show sometime. When he does—I take him, too."

"I'll get ready," said Parmalee. "We'll go together."

"No." Hawk shook his head, standing up. "I go alone."

"What? You're goddam crazy." The old man stared at Hawk, blue eyes blazing. "Brava already left you fer dead once."

"Alone, or not at all," said Hawk. "I took your people with me the last time. That fouled it. Besides, Brava an' Vansittart are mine: I owe them."

"There's likely to be three," said Parmalee. "Can you handle that?"

"I can handle it," said Hawk. "I want to handle it. On my own."

"Like I said," grunted Parmalee. "The last time you tangled with them you got left fer a corpse."

"But I rose up," said Hawk, gravely. "And now I'm gonna crucify them."

14

BLANCO CANYON was a vast rift in the bedrock of the Jornado del Muerto range. Two to three miles long, it was approached through a narrow, rock-walled ravine that opened suddenly into the main body of the canyon. The sides spread out in a fan so that from Hawk's vantage point on the rimrock the opening assumed the shape of a massive Y. The walls spread apart, then began to curve gradually round in a long semi-circle that was bisected by a second entrance. It was easy to see how the place had got its name, for the stone was a curious whitish shade, almost chalky, reflecting the sun so that in sections it shone like pure snow. Interlacing the high, steep walls were side gulleys and smaller box canyons, hidden in shadow. A stream ran diagonally across the centre, spilling down from the north-eastern wall and disappearing into a cleft on the south side. The floor of the canyon was thick with grass and scruboaks, interspersed with bushes. The foliage looked dense, impenetrable except where a network of narrow trails cut through the green like veins in a cheese.

Hawk guessed that there were side trails leading out from the peripheral splits: it was easy to see how a posse could lose its quarry there.

He scanned the canyon, riding slowly along the rim, but saw nothing. He turned the black horse around and went down the ridge, coming to the trail leading out from Green Springs.

There was no sign of movement. The dust covering the trail was undisturbed, and the town was a faint blur in the distance, overhung with a thin layer of smoke from Parmalee's mine. Hawk rode for the entrance to Blanco Canyon, steering his mount through the cholla and mesquite flanking the main trail so that he would not leave tracks.

He reached the opening of the ravine and halted, remembering the last time he had entered a place like this. Remembering what the Brava gang had done to him there. He eased the cut-down Meteor from its holster and cocked the scattergun. Then, holding the shotgun canted against his right shoulder, he walked the pony into the darkness.

The walls of the ravine stretched up on either side, narrow and gloomy, overhung with roots and thick growths of ivy.

He reached the exit point and halted again. The interior of Blanco Canyon was filled with light, the walls trapping the sun and reflecting it down over the dense undergrowth. They looked even higher from this level: sheer cliffs that seemd to stretch upwards until they touched the clear blue of the sky to join with the drifting shapes of white clouds. The side gulleys were like the smiling jaws of skulls, dark splits against bone white; reminders of mortality.

And Brava and Vansittart could be hidden in any one of them. Waiting. Watching. Holding Hawk in their gunsights.

He dismounted, holstering the scatter-gun and tugging the Winchester from the saddle scabbard. He levered a shell into the breech and led the black horse out of the shadows of the ravine into the brilliant sunlight.

Growing close against the left-side wall of the canyon was a thick stand of scrub-boak with a declivity immediately behind. The indentation of the rock and the density of the trees provided an area of protected shadow. Hawk took the black horse inside and fastened a hobble to the stallion's forelegs. Then he wrapped a length of cloth around its muzzle, gagging it so that it could not snicker a warning or a greeting to any approaching horses.

After that he drifted out through the trees and took up position just inside the canyon's entrance.

Time went by. Slowly, as though teasing him with doubt that his plan had worked. The canyon was hot—got warmer—and the lush grass was heavy with the murmur of insects and the song of birds. He slumped against the gnarled bole of an oak, waiting.

Then, from inside the ravine, there came the sound of hoofbeats. Of a horse driven hard.

He stood up, moving forwards to a place just beside the nearest pathway.

And watched as a bay gelding came panting from the ravine. Sweat lathered the animal's mouth and neck, and when it halted it let its head droop, panting. It was ridden by a man in a black suit, his dark hair empty of a hat and plastered against his forehead with sweat.

Hawk ran to grab the bridle, dragging the gelding's head even farther down as he slammed a boot against the left forelimb so that the tired pony squealed once and tilted over to the side.

Hawk yanked it all the way down, pitching it over as he thrust the muzzle of the Winchester deep into Father Durant's belly so that the priest gasped and doubled over, his feet leaving the stirrups as the force of the blow carried him backwards from the saddle.

Horse and holy father went down together, the gelding sideways, Durant on his back.

Hawk swung the reins over the pony's head and looped them fast around the fetlocks. The horse grunted and stretched out, too weary to protest. Durant curled into a tight ball, hands pressed tight against his stomach, a thin splatter of vomit coughing from between his groaning lips.

The groaning stopped when Hawk jammed the muzzle of the rifle tight against the priest's mouth and said:

"I done my turn confessing, Father. You want to try it?"

Durant's pale face got paler still. All the colour went away so that only the bruised impression around his lips and the dark shadows under his eyes gave contrast to the waxen pallor of his skin.

"You lied to me." He sounded almost shocked. "You entered the confessional booth and lied to me."

"Reckon you done your share." Hawk eased the Winchester a few inches from the priest's face and cocked the hammer. "Now tell me the truth."

"Oh, God!" Durant's features crumpled into a parody of his former calm. Heavy tears burst from his eyes, trickling down his cheeks as he rubbed at his stomach and mouth together. "I never wanted it like this."

"Nor me," said Hawk. "I never wanted to get pegged out an' left to die. I never wanted that girl to shoot at me. But that's how it happens sometimes. The difference between us is that I see that; you don't. But when it happens, you gotta face it an' handle it, any way you can. How'd you try to handle it, Father? By stealin' Parmalee's gold?"

"I didn't want to," moaned the priest. "God knows, I didn't want to. Listen, I'll tell you everything."

"Talk fast," said Hawk. "Brava and Vansittart ain't gonna wait too long."

"She was my sister," said Durant. "Her full name was Johanna Durant. Mine is Jonas Durant. We were born in St. Louis. Wealthy. I always wanted to be a priest, and Johanna was always wild. She got pregnant when she was fifteen and ran away from home. I was already studying in the seminary in St. Joseph, so all I heard was what my parents told me in letters. It seems the father was a local boy—Cole Vansittart. He left Johanna when she asked him to marry her, but she never gave up on the idea. She never went home, either.

"I guess she became a prostitute round about then, because I didn't see her for the next few years. My parents got letters from her from time to time. It sounded like she was following Vansittart around the country. Sounded like he'd become an outlaw.

"Then we met on the stagecoach coming to Green Springs. I couldn't believe it! She was changed so much I barely recognized her. She told me she'd caught up with Vansittart in Durango and he'd promised to live with her when he had enough money. She believed him, so she agreed to help him.

"Then he came to see her in Green

Springs. As soon as he knew I was the priest, he worked out his plan.

"They both came to me. Laughing in my own church! They said that if I didn't help them they'd tell everyone my sister was a whore. Vansittart said he'd kill me."

The tears got larger and the priest forgot about his bruised belly as he wiped them clear. Hawk waited.

"I was guilty of pride and fear," said Durant. "I didn't want the town to know my own sister had become a common woman. And I was afraid of what Cole would do. I agreed to help them."

"So you listened to the guards' confessions," murmured Hawk, "an' then picked out the best load to steal."

Durant nodded. "God forgive me! But yes, I couldn't bear the embarrassment. And Cole promised no one would get killed."

"What else?" Hawk asked; cold. "You was in for a share."

"I planned to send it to the Church," whined the priest. "I would have given half to Johanna, so that she might regain a decent life; and the rest I would have sent to my Mission."

"And now you don't have any of it." Hawk moved back, motioning for Durant to stand up. "No gold. No sister. No church."

"I still have my God," said Durant. "He has not deserted me."

"Go find him," said Hawk, slipping the reins from the gelding's forelocks. "An' nor will I."

Durant moved out from the ravine with Hawk trailing close behind. On foot. Down in the grass where his movement wouldn't be noticed under the higher movement of the bay pony.

The priest steered out towards the centre of Blanco Canyon and then cut off to the south, following a game trail that led towards one of the peripheral gulleys.

He was two hundred yards out, riding through a stand of scruboak that hid the gunfighter's position, when the first shot rang out.

It entered his chest at the apex of his

black vest, just below the white of the dog-collar. It went in through the soft tissue at the base of the throat, tearing into the muscle of the neck so that his head jerked forwards, his tongue protruding from between his gaping lips. It struck his shoulderblade and deflected downwards, ripping into a lung so that the head snapped back and the tongue was abruptly covered with the blood spouting from his mouth.

The second shot took him as he slumped backwards. It was aimed lower, targeted in by the direction and strike point of the first. It caught Durant in the belly, bursting through the fragile overlay of flesh and muscle to pierce his stomach and ricochet off the pelvic girdle into the priest's groin.

Durant screamed and began to slide sideways off the bay gelding. For a moment, his hands lifted clear of the reins. The right traced the sign of the cross against his bloody chest; the left thrust the leather strips towards Hawk.

The gunfighter darted out from the

cover of the trees. Grabbed the reins from the priest's hand and tugged Durant's feet clear of the stirrups. The priest fell down on the ground, the force bursting fresh thickets of blood from his mouth and belly and neck.

Hawk took hold of the saddle, holding the reins back as he hung down the side of the gelding and smashed the stock of his Winchester backwards against the pony's ribs.

The horse squealed and ran forwards. Hawk draped both hands over the saddle-horn, holding his head down as the panicked animal galloped straight for the cut that had exposed the two riflemen.

His feet bounced on the rough ground, and his arms ached, sparks of pain dancing up from the stiffened fingers of his gloved left hand; from the crooked elbow of his right arm.

The gelding reached the entrance to the cut and Hawk let go. He rolled clear, thudding through the high grass until he struck a scruboak and came to rest, twisting over on to his belly with the Winchester thrust out in front.

The horse went on running until two shots cut it down. Dropping it like a log across the slanting trail that led upwards towards the southern edge of Blanco Canyon.

For a long time there was nothing but the sound of the insects and the birds. Hawk bellied down under the oak, grateful for the shade, waiting.

Then Luis Brava and Cole Vansittart came out from the split. Both men led horses with their left hands, the rights clutching handguns. Brava's was one of the cross-hung Colts, the ivory grip hidden beneath his pudgy fingers; Vansittart was carrying the Smith & Wesson. Hawk watched them come down into the bowl of the canyon and take their mounts north, along a thin path that skirted the base of the cliffs.

He followed them, moving like a thief in the afternoon sun.

They moved cautiously at first, gaining confidence as the canyon continued quiet;

speeding their movements and beginning to speak as the silence assured them of safety.

"We got the last one," said Vansittart. "Ain't no one gonna take that from us."

"It's a sin to kill a priest," replied Brava. "We must make penance."

Vansittart chuckled. "You can buy all the candles you want, Luis. Gold candles."

The Mexican nodded, beginning to smile. "*Si*. I guess I can. I'll put some up for Father Durant."

"Yeah." Vansittart laughed out loud. "An' put one up for his sister."

Hawk followed them to where a gulley came down in a spill of sun-washed stone on to an area surrounded by oaks and bushes. He waited outside until they had manhandled the last gold wagon down on to the flat ground. Went on waiting as they fetched mules out from the split and hitched them to the wagon.

Then he stepped out into the light with

the Winchester cocked and angled at a point mid-way between the two men.

Luis Brava was dressed in the same yellow shirt he had worn the first time Hawk had seen him. The bandoliers draped across his chest emphasized the swell of his belly and the yellow handles of the forwards-butted pistols on his hips. Cole Vansittart was wearing a dark blue shirt, the colour crossed by the fastenings of his shoulder rig. The butt of the Smith & Wesson protruded starkly from the holster under his sweat-stained left arm.

"I told you I'd see you again," snarled Hawk. "I told you I'd kill you."

Brava dropped his arms across his waist, but then Vansittart halted his draw by saying, "No need to kill him, Luis. Not now."

"*Por que?*" Brava grunted, his little eyes battening down into porcine slits. "He killed Federico."

"He took the gold, too," said Vansittart. "Ain't that right, feller?"

"Name's Hawk," said the gunfighter. "Jared Hawk."

"The name's not important," said Vansittart. "The gold is. Was you found it, wasn't it?"

Hawk nodded, not taking his eyes off either man.

"Yeah. I killed Braco an' Strother. Johanna too."

"No great loss," said Vansittart. "Pity is you took it all back to Parmalee. That *is* what you did, ain't it?"

"Yeah. What I was hired to do." Hawk went on watching. "Mostly when I promise something, I carry it through."

"There's a whole lotta gold here," said the Southerner. "Enough to share."

"Parmalee said there was three thousand on each wagon," said Hawk. "That's a lot."

"Enough to split three ways," said Vansittart. "Think about it. You'd still get yore money from Parmalee."

"No." Hawk shook his head; a barely perceptible movement that never once allowed his eyes to move from the two outlaws. "He pays me on results. Your bodies are the results."

"So we don't have a deal?" asked Vansittart. "You ain't prepared to listen to sense."

"Like I said," Hawk rasped, "I keep my promises. Especially to myself. An' I promised I'd kill you."

"Crazy," grunted Vansittart. "Real crazy."

As he said it, he threw himself to the side, right hand stretching across his chest to pluck the S&W clear of the holster. Brava followed his cue, lifting both pistols clear of his waist with the hammers snapping back as his fingers tightened on the triggers.

Hawk dropped the Winchester. He might have taken one of them with the rifle, but the lever action would have slowed him after that, maybe enough for them to kill him. He preferred to rely on the handguns for close range work.

The Meteor slid clear of the holster while the rifle was still falling. The familiar pistol grip slotted smoothly into his right hand as his gloved left came up to clasp the shortened barrel and hold it down against the massive kick of the heavy Ten gauge shot. Vansittart was still dropping to the left, though Brava stayed upright, lifting his Colts as though in slow motion as the adrenalin coursed through Hawk's body and seemed to slow time.

He knew that Brava had a better chance of hitting him because he was standing and aiming, while Vansittart could be put off by the fall that was taking him out of range.

So he turned the shotgun slightly to the right and squeezed the trigger with the stubby muzzle pointed towards the Mexican.

The Meteor detonated a terrifying blast of shot out from the swirl of black powder smoke and lancing flame.

At that range it picked Luis Brava up from the ground while he was still thumbing the hammers of his Colts. It tore away the right side of his face, stripping off the flesh so that the skull beneath was suddenly exposed, the teeth along the line of his jaw shining yellow, the socket of his eye opening to drop the orb down over his empty cheek. He lifted up and back, a sideways scream gusting from his split mouth along with a massive fountain of blood. His guns blasted twin shots into the sky and he crashed down on his back with half his yellow shirt abruptly dark, crimson with the blood pouring from his ghastly face.

Hawk dropped the shotgun and slid the Colt clear of the holster as he pivoted on his right heel and let himself fall to that side.

Vansittart's shot passed a half inch over his side. He could feel the wind of its passage as he triggered his own gun at the Southerner.

He hit the ground with a second bullet blasting towards the man in the black suit. The first spanged off the rock behind Vansittart, ricocheting away down the gulley. The second ploughed splinters from the wagon: Vansittart moved fast.

Already he was under the wagon. Now moving behind its cover. Shouting at Hawk.

"This is crazy! We can split this. Share

three thousand dollars in pure gold. That's enough for any two men! What do you say?"

"All right." Hawk lifted to his knees behind a boulder. "How do I trust you though?"

"I never wanted to peg you out," called Vansittart. "It was Luis wanted that. I figgered you'd get free somehow."

Like Johanna? Hawk thought, and said: "All right, what do we do?"

"Holster our guns," called the Southerner. "Then stand up. Together, on the count of three. You call it."

"You got a deal," said Hawk, thumbing fresh loads into the Colt. "Like you say."

"Don't try nothing," called the outlaw. "With this much gold to split between us it ain't worth it."

"No," called Hawk. "It ain't. One!"

He settled the Colt in the holster, testing the slide of oiled metal against polished leather.

"Two!"

He slid gently to the edge of the

boulder, balancing on the balls of his feet, left hand touching the rock.

"Three!"

He stood up as Cole Vansittart came lifted upright from behind the wagon with the S&W spiking flame over the tarpaulin. His movement carried him clear of the boulder. Clear of the shot. He powered sideways, firing at the feet of the mules, rather than at the outlaw.

The bullet landed between the legs of the forward animals, ploughing dirt in a spattering fountain that struck their bellies and hindquarters. They snorted a shrill protest and pulled forwards, plunging away from the sudden explosion in a surge of nervous power.

It left Vansittart exposed, his gun hand thrown up by the violent forwards motion of the wagon. Hawk fired again from a prone position, the bullet angling up to hit the Southerner at the midpoint of his ribs.

It entered Vansittart's stomach and ploughed on through the entrails to strike against a hindwards rib and deflect out through his back. Along the way it ruptured a kidney and burst several arteries. Vansittart fell backwards with blood pumping from the front of his shirt and a wider gouting spraying from his back.

Hawk rolled, going on firing as the Southerner thudded against the ground and fought to lift his gun to return a shot. None came, because Hawk's bullets rammed awful holes through Vansittart's body. The second, striking as the man went down, struck his groin, ripping up through his genitals to deflect off the pelvic girdle and lodge just under his heart. The third and fourth completed the ruin of his body, one bursting his heart and the other smashing through the right eye as he screamed and jerked upright under the impact.

Vansittart's shirt was stained dark with blood. More spilled from his body, joining the flow of urine and faeces loosened from him by Hawk's bullets. His face erupted outwards, a pulpy mixture of eye and brain matter joining the fragments of bone gusting from his skull. He slumped back, the Smith & Wesson dropping from his dead fingers with most of the chambers still unfired.

Hawk climbed to his feet, snapping the spent shells from the cylinder of the Colt. He thumbed fresh loads into place and holstered the revolver. Then he picked up the shotgun. Reloaded, and dropped it back into the sling.

There were flies gathering over the bodies as he calmed the mules and lifted on to the seat.

As he rode away, dark specks began to show across the sky and a coyote howled from somewhere down Blanco Canyon.

By the time he collected the black horse and went out through the ravine the specks had become distinct; vultures moving in on fresh pickings; and the eerie sounds of the coyotes were much closer.

Scavengers moving in on easy meat.

He began to calculate his earnings, confident that Parmalee would take his word for the killings. If not, then all the old man needed do was ride out to Blanco

Canyon and check what the scavengers had left. A thousand each, he had been promised, which added up to four grand. Five if the dead priest got counted in. It was a lot of money: when he reached Valverde he would send it all back east. Back to the farm, to Jamey and his mother.

He glanced over his shoulder, staring at the bulky outline of the tarpaulin-covered gold. That was a lot, too.

More than most men saw in a lifetime.

Maybe even worth dying for.

Then he shook his head, correcting himself as he thought about all the lives that had gone to bring the gold back.

And grinned. "Just fool's gold," he murmured. And headed the mules in the direction of Green Springs.

Other titles in the
Linford Western Series:

FARGO: MASSACRE RIVER
by John Benteen

Fargo spurred his horse to the edge of the road. Its right hind hoof slipped perilously over the edge as he forced it around the wagon. Ahead he saw Jade Ching riding hard, bent low in her saddle. Fargo rammed home his spurs and drove his mount up to her. The ambushers up ahead had now blocked the road. Fargo's convoy was a jumble, a perfect target for the insurgents' weapons!

SUNDANCE:
DEATH IN THE LAVA
by John Benteen

The land echoed with the thundering hoofs of Modoc ponies. In minutes they swooped down and captured the wagon train and its cargo of gold. But now the halfbreed they called Sundance was going after it, and he swore nothing would stand in his way—not Indian savagery of the vicious gunfighters of the town named Hell.

FARGO: THE SHARPSHOOTERS
by John Benteen

The Canfield clan, thirty strong, were raising hell in Texas. One of them had shot a Texas Ranger, and the Rangers had to bring in the killer. The last thing they wanted though was a feud. Fargo, arrested for gunrunning, was promised he could go free if he would walk into the Canfield's lair and bring out the killer. And Fargo was tough enough to hold his own against the whole clan.

SUNDANCE: OVERKILL
by John Benteen

Sundance's reputation as a fighting man had spread from Canada to Mexico, from the Mississippi to the Pacific. There was no job too tough for the halfbreed to handle. So when a wealthy banker's daughter was kidnapped by the Cheyenne, he offered Sundance $10,000 to rescue the girl. Sundance became a moving target for both the U.S. Cavalry and his own blood brothers.

DAY OF THE COMANCHEROS
by Steven C. Lawrence

Their very name struck terror into men's hearts—the Comancheros, a savage army of cutthroats who swept across Texas, leaving behind a bloodstained trail of robbery and murder. When Tom Slattery stumbled on some of their slaughtered victims, he found only one survivor, young Anna Peterson. With a cavalry escort, he set out to bring the murderers to justice.

SUNDANCE: SILENT ENEMY
by John Benteen

Both the Indians and the U.S. Cavalry were being victimized. A lone crazed Cheyenne was on a personal war path against both sides and neither brigades of bluecoats nor tribes of braves could end his reign of terror. They needed to pit one man against one crazed Indian. That man was Sundance.